What the critics are saying...

"...a fantastic read...if you're in the mood for a steamy story with lots of intriguing sex, this is certainly one you won't want to miss." ~ *Susan Mobley, Romantic Times Magazine*

Five Stars "...This is quite possibly the funniest, sexiest, most heart-warming story I've ever read!" ~ *Amy L. Turpin, Timeless Tales Reviews*

"...Sahara Kelly takes readers on a walk on the wild side with this magical world of sex expert Djinn...One will only hope more is to come featuring this unique, fantasy lamp." ~ *Miriam, Love Romances*

"...While filled with plenty of erotic encounters and fantasies, this story also has a plot that captures the interest of its reader. So many erotic tales are so focused on the eroticism they leave out this essential element to any good story. While traveling between different times and worlds, the reader is drawn into this fantasy world and it makes the eroticism that more powerful and moving." ~ *Katy, A Romance Review*

Sahara Kelly

ALANA'S MAGIC LAMP

GUARDIANS OF TIME

ELLORA'S CAVE
ROMANTICA PUBLISHING

An Ellora's Cave Romantica Publication

www.ellorascave.com

Guardians of Time: Alana's Magic Lamp

ISBN # 1419950479
ALL RIGHTS RESERVED.
Guardians of Time: Alana's Magic Lamp
Copyright© 2002 Sahara Kelly
Edited by: Jennifer Martin
Cover art by: Syneca

Electronic book Publication: September, 2002
Trade paperback Publication: May, 2005

Excerpt from *The Sun God's Woman*
Copyright © Sahara Kelly, 2002

Warning:

The following material contains graphic sexual content meant for mature readers. *Alana's Magic Lamp* has been rated *E-rotic* by a minimum of three independent reviewers.

Ellora's Cave Publishing offers three levels of Romantica™ reading entertainment: S (S-ensuous), E (E-rotic), and X (X-treme).

S-*ensuous* love scenes are explicit and leave nothing to the imagination.

E-*rotic* love scenes are explicit, leave nothing to the imagination, and are high in volume per the overall word count. In addition, some E-rated titles might contain fantasy material that some readers find objectionable, such as bondage, submission, same sex encounters, forced seductions, etc. E-rated titles are the most graphic titles we carry; it is common, for instance, for an author to use words such as "fucking", "cock", "pussy", etc., within their work of literature.

X-*treme* titles differ from E-rated titles only in plot premise and storyline execution. Unlike E-rated titles, stories designated with the letter X tend to contain controversial subject matter not for the faint of heart.

Also by Sahara Kelly:

Alana's Magic Lamp
Guardians of Time

To Chickiebabe, Bosslady and the Wizard - happiness is having a critique group that is also slightly warped. To Jennifer – profound thanks for taking a chance on this one.

Chapter One

"They're dicks!"

"I've been telling you that for years."

"No, no...I'm not talking about men, here, look at this—they look like dicks."

Janet Beatty pointed at an article on a table in the far corner of the room and grabbed her friend's arm.

"Janet, give me a break here. You're always talking about men and this is the first table with some decent jewelry I've found all afternoon."

Alana West sighed as she eased her arm away from Janet's fingers. Her other hand held her tumble of hair away from her face as she gazed critically over the display on the white cloth. This was a pretty good estate sale, all things considered, the coffee was strong and the cookies were fresh. The owners had obviously contacted a lot of their friends because there was more selection here than could be offered by a single seller.

Alana knew whereof she spoke—it was her job to analyze and authenticate small *objects d'art* with a special attention to seventeenth and eighteenth century jewelry. She was still hoping for an undiscovered treasure—a special miniature perhaps or the perfect cameo which would bolster the reputation of her small store and lead to bigger and more profitable assignments.

Looking up she realized her friend was watching her impatiently.

"Just because you're Miss I'm-Not-Distracted-by-Sex, there is no need to act all snotty with me! I bought you your first vibrator, remember?"

"Jeez, Jan, keep your voice down. I'd rather not announce things like that to the whole room, if you don't mind!" She frowned at her best friend since high school who was giving her the "yeah, right" look.

"Not everything is about sex, Janet—I happen to be really enjoying this sale. There's some great stuff here..."

"None of which is a good substitute for a warm body."

Alana sighed. They'd had this discussion on numerous occasions, in various stages of sobriety, and the conclusion was pretty much the same. Janet loved men and sex, large quantities of each, and Alana had yet to find a guy who could bring her that mind-blowing orgasm that magazines, and Janet, continually told her she was supposed to be having. She'd cancelled her subscription to the magazines and given up on men, but she couldn't quite bring herself to shut Janet up.

"Seriously, Al, I'm not at all fixated here. You have to come and see this thing..." and she tugged Alana's arm again impatiently.

"Oh okay. I don't see anything that really catches the eye here anyway. I can always come back." And with good grace, she gave in to the urging and followed Janet toward a darkened corner of the room.

The sunlight hadn't made it to this table, so it was quite amazing that Janet had even noticed the unusual artifact sitting off to one side. A man was standing next to the table, using a soft cloth to rub a brass candlestick to a deep rich glow. He was clearly the owner or the seller at least, of the articles on show.

He turned as the two women approached and a gentle smile crossed his lips. Alana felt mesmerized for a second as his unusually dark eyes met hers. A chill danced over her skin and the hairs on the back of her neck tingled.

"Good afternoon, Mademoiselles." He bowed his head elegantly. "Are you looking for anything in particular?"

A slight accent, which Alana couldn't place, seemed in keeping with his slightly exotic appearance. There were silver streaks threading through the long dark hair, neatly tied back for this occasion. His moustache and goatee were speckled with gray, but his suit was expensively cut, impeccably pressed, and his slender hands knew how to cradle valuable artifacts. He could have been thirty, or a very young fifty – he had that ageless quality about him. His skin was smooth enough, however, to put him closer to the first age, but his eyes... They held the secrets of eternity. A gallery owner perhaps, wondered Alana, feeling an odd excitement low in her belly.

"We were interested in *that*..." blurted out Janet, pointing at the item which stood by itself in an empty area.

"We were? Good God," breathed Alana, seeing for the first time what had gotten Janet so hot and bothered.

It looked to be made of wood — some rich polished mahogany-type wood — and was about ten inches tall. Wider at the bottom than the top, the vessel or whatever it was had a plug in the neck that might well have been a leather-covered cork. There were some small decorations around its neck, which Alana believed could be pure gold — even from this distance there was a certain patina that gave it away. But the eye-catching handles were what gave this piece its distinctive appearance.

As Janet had so accurately noted, they looked like dicks! On either side, two thick handles curved gently from the body to the top—they were ridged and carved to look just like the real thing—right down to the base where a full sac lay in an amazingly life-like fashion against the bottom of the vessel and the table. The effect was so real that Alana felt an almost irresistible urge to run her hands down from neck to base and back up again.

Blushing, she backed away slightly.

"Ah yes…" said the man. "You have noticed one of my more interesting pieces…" He reached over and picked up the vessel, carefully cradling it in his hands. "It is made of the finest woods, and is from the estate of Dr. Maurice Willis, a renowned collector of unusual pieces from the Middle East."

Alana couldn't take her eyes off it as he turned and rotated it to show her the skill of the craftsman.

"What is it?" she croaked, finding her voice oddly rough.

"It is a pleasure vessel."

"Oooh, that sounds like my kind of antique," laughed Janet reaching out.

Surprisingly, the man held it away from Janet's fingers.

"If you will permit, I would prefer that this be handled only by those who are serious in its purchase. I believe that you, young lady, are such a one?" His midnight gaze rested on Alana.

She nodded uncomfortably, fingers itching to hold the piece.

"You are? Well, this is a first," muttered Janet, puzzled at Alana's absent gaze.

"This vessel, and others like it, was used to hold the oil of the Blue Lotus—much prized in ancient times. It is said that the oil could be used to produce stimulation, arousal and ecstasy. It was used extensively..."

"...by the ancient Egyptians. Yes, I know. It was rumored that Tutankhamen's tomb held Blue Lotus petals which is why historians revised their first opinion that it was only a decorative flower..." Alana held out her hands slowly, answering the call of this strange vessel. *Hold me, touch me!*

Raising an eyebrow at Alana's evident knowledge of the subject, he nodded.

"Quite right, Mademoiselle. You are most well-read on the antiquities, yes?"

Keeping her eyes on the bottle, Alana absently brushed off his compliment.

"The discovery of the lotus in the tomb led to a revival of Egyptian jewelry in the 1930's. I have to know about things like that. It's my job. Oh please, may I hold it?"

He placed it carefully into Alana's hands and stepped back. Janet asked him a question about another piece, but Alana couldn't concentrate on anything besides the feel of the artifact in her hands. It pulsed as if it was a living, breathing thing. The wood was warm and velvety to her touch, and as she gave in to temptation and ran the tip of her index finger up one of the handles to its very tip, she could swear she heard a deep sigh of pleasure.

"I'll take it!" She surprised herself with the emphatic statement. This wasn't how it was supposed to go. She was supposed to inquire about provenance, negotiate a price, perhaps go away and come back again—she knew all the rules and was breaking every one of them. She just had to have it. It was hers.

At that moment, when the words left her lips, she could have sworn that the handles twitched!

* * * * *

"So what'll it be…pizza? Chinese? Or are you up for Italian?"

Alana carefully steered her Jeep out onto the highway and headed for home. "Actually, Jan, I think I'm gonna pass this time…" She flicked a quick glance in the rear view mirror, telling herself that she was being a good driver and monitoring the road behind her, when what she really wanted to do was make sure the carefully packed box was still safe behind her back seat.

"You feeling okay?" asked Janet, a worried frown crossing her face. "You've been awfully quiet since you bought the dickpot. Of course, if I'd just spent twelve hundred bucks like it was nothing, I'd probably be a bit sick too." She shook her head.

"It's just a little headache—all those musty tablecloths we went through were probably covered in dust. But Jan, trust me on this. I got a bargain on that vessel. If it is really Middle Eastern, then I'd put it at somewhere around four to five thousand years old, which is unheard of for an artifact like that. So show a little respect and don't call it a dickpot, will you?"

Janet frowned again. "I didn't think wood could last that long unless it was fossilized?"

"It's certainly very unusual to find something that old, that's for sure, although there were some in tomb finds.

I'm going on what I remember about decorative techniques and symbols, and some of those around the top of the vessel are unique to Middle Egypt. They were copied in the Regency era during the big run on all things Egyptian, that's how I know about them."

"So how do you know this isn't a Regency copy?"

"I don't—not until I examine it more closely, but—don't laugh at me—have you ever had a really, *really* strong feeling about something as soon as you touched it?" She glanced quickly over at Janet to see if she appreciated the seriousness of the question. "Because I got one when I picked that up—it was like it was meant to be mine. It felt…I don't know…*right* in my hands."

"Oh it's happened with a couple of guys," Janet grinned, willing to accept Alana's word. In all the years they'd known each other, Janet couldn't remember a time when Alana had acted in such a spontaneous and out-of-character fashion. She turned back to the road and gazed ahead, trusting that her friend knew what she was doing.

Alana drove on autopilot. Her mind was still on that magical moment when the vessel had moved within her grasp. The handles had jumped slightly, and she could have sworn that for a split second she felt one of them throb beneath her fingers.

She knew she wasn't given to fanciful notions, nor was she on any type of medication, but these were feelings she'd never had before. She was looking forward to getting back to the safety of her own apartment, where she could examine them, and the vessel, in the peace and security of her own surroundings. She couldn't wait to drop Janet off and get home—alone.

* * * * *

The door slammed with a comforting thunk behind her, and Alana heaved a sigh of relief as she locked it and tossed her jacket and purse on the hallstand. Carrying her treasure carefully, she eased it onto the kitchen table and pulled the shredded straw packaging away.

It gleamed in the late day sunlight as she raised it out from its nest. Holding it carefully to the light, she turned it this way and that, being careful not to touch the handles. She looked for maker's marks, insignia, strange designs, in fact any indication as to who might have made it or where it came from.

There was nothing. Nothing but a wonderful, exquisitely carved, smooth and inviting piece of art. Perhaps there would be something on one or two of her favorite antique websites—she should certainly spend some time researching it.

It was still a gorgeous piece, no matter what the origin, so Alana wandered around her apartment looking for the right spot to put it. She checked the dining area, but it was quite formal and simple—something like this needed a better display. The living room was chock-full of books, a DVD and CD library, and her puzzle collection. Ignoring a little voice that sounded a lot like Janet saying "Look at this, the room of a perennial virgin!" she wandered on down the hall to her bedroom. Just as she stepped inside, a wave of dizziness swept over her and she reached out for the footboard to her sleigh bed. Catching sight of herself in the long wall mirror, she realized she held the vessel so that both handles were pressed to her breasts—breasts that were now tingling and throbbing. She jerked the vessel away and stared at it. If she didn't know better, she'd say she just got a shock from it!

Alana's eyes fell on the tall plant stand next to the mirror. It was right in front of a fanciful niche stencil that Alana had done in her "Martha Stewart" phase, and as soon as she saw it, she knew that was the spot. It took ten seconds to remove the small bud vase with its silk roses and replace it with the vessel. Stepping back, Alana nodded approvingly.

Another wave of dizziness tingled over her — what was with this? "Shower," she thought to herself, "then food. It's gotta be a sugar level imbalance." Toeing off her sneakers and unzipping her jeans, Alana dodged into the kitchen, grabbed a cold soda, and headed for the shower, snagging her favorite old bathrobe along the way.

Half an hour and one refreshing shower later, Alana emerged back into her room, toweling off her hair. She paused for a moment, then sniffed — and sniffed again. She could smell a fragrance — not perfume exactly, but not incense either.

"Must be George going overboard on the candles again," she said to herself, thinking with distaste about her neighbor two doors down whom she had mistakenly dated and stupidly fucked when he had first moved in last year. She yanked her hairbrush savagely through her unruly curls as if to punish herself for being such an idiot.

"No finesse, didn't even wait until I'd made coffee to get my pants off. Damn near took me standing up in the kitchen, about two hours before I was ready, and Janet wonders why I don't like sex?" Alana harrumphed at her reflection. "It's a miracle the species survives when there are men like George around!"

A quiet laugh breezed around the room behind her.

She spun quickly, clutching the lapels of her robe, but saw no one.

"That's it, no more thinking about sex," she said firmly to herself. "I'm certainly going downhill when I start hearing things!"

Unwillingly, her brushing movements paused as her eyes fell on the vessel. She sniffed again.

"Damn, I wonder if there's something inside that's smelling." Visions of dead things decomposing flashed through her mind, and it was with a very careful hand that she gripped the plug and gave it a tug. Nothing happened.

Getting a better grip on both vessel and plug, she pulled again. Still nothing.

"Damn, this is in here tightly..." She held the vessel close and peered at the plug to see if there was a seal, but she couldn't find anything that would prevent the plug from coming out.

Grabbing it firmly, she pressed it to her stomach for strength and gave the hardest pull she could manage on the plug. Nothing budged an inch.

Flexing her fingers, she obeyed a strange whim and sniffed them. There it was. The fragrance that had been permeating her room was definitely coming from the vessel. Then she remembered — Blue Lotus oil. Was it possible there was still some in there? After all these years? If there was, it had probably been added recently. There was no way fragranced oil could have survived thousands of years, was there?

Stumped, Alana sat on the side of the bed holding the vessel and gazing at it. Giving in to temptation she ran her fingers up one of the handles, and this time circled the tip with her finger before following the shaft back down to the base, where she caressed the rounded sac. A distinct moan floated around her.

She jumped and dropped the vessel on the bed, wiping her suddenly sweaty palms on her thighs.

Her body felt very warm, and her skin began to feel tight, sensitive, over-stretched. In fact, the soft cotton of her old robe was becoming irritating to her nerve endings. She hurriedly shrugged it off her shoulders and let it fall to the floor, unconcerned that she was naked beneath.

She swallowed, throat dry and tongue sticking somewhere in her mouth. "This is nuts..." she breathed, as her body's sensations became even more pronounced. Her breasts began throbbing in earnest, and she couldn't help but watch as her nipples puckered and hardened as if suckled by an unseen mouth.

She gasped as she realized a drop of her juices was slowly dripping down the inside of one thigh. She was totally and completely aroused—and she was alone! What was happening to her? Her clit was beginning to ache and she felt a strange urge to push her hips forward, toward the vessel. She stepped closer, and the nearer she got, the more intense the feelings became. Her hands rose, blindly seeking out her own nipples to relieve the aching pressure. She caught sight of herself in the mirror and moaned. What was she *doing*? Who was this wanton woman fondling her breasts and watching her own arousal? She needed *something* and her eyes turned again to the vessel. She knew now that the handles had moved—they were standing much further away from the vessel and were hard and straight—the soft curves of the mahogany had become rigid ironwood.

Unable to stop herself, she reached for the vessel and brought it to her now dripping pussy. She felt the throb as she touched one handle to her clit, and sighed aloud as she rubbed the head over herself, soaking the handle and her fingers in the process with her astoundingly abundant moisture. It was so smooth and felt so perfect against her superheated flesh. Her knees buckled as she felt the first shivers of her approaching orgasm, and the vessel slipped from her wet fingers...

"Oh God, no. Not now," she cried, grabbing one handle firmly with her hand and sliding the other handle back over her aroused clitoris. It was a matter of moments before her shivers began again, and each movement she made seemed to ratchet the tension in her body up a notch. Her hips thrust, her toes curled and her breasts became swollen and tipped with dark sensitive nipples. A quick glimpse in her mirror showed her a woman writhing toward the heights of ecstasy. Her hands were moving so fast that the vessel was merely a blur—one handle sliding up and down though her fingers and the other sliding up and down through her swollen and sensitive flesh.

Just when she thought she would die if she didn't come—it happened. An orgasmic explosion racked her body with the most exquisite tremors, and every muscle she had spasmed for what seemed like hours. A sob erupted from her throat and she fell back onto the bed and into oblivion.

Chapter Two

Alana came slowly back to consciousness feeling better than she could ever remember feeling before. Her body was relaxed, sated, and felt as boneless as a slug. She stretched her arms high above her head and smiled as she opened her eyes. God, that had been good...

She froze. Rising from her dewy skin was a soft blue vapor, trailing this way and that, softly caressing her and making her pores tingle. It felt wonderful, but it was blue vapor. Blue vapor should not be in her bedroom swathing her body like some weird Hollywood special effect. She shut her eyes again, determined that it would be gone when she opened them. Turning her head to the side, she slowly opened one eye.

A wickedly handsome face smiled at her.

"Oh God..."

She turned the other way and opened the same eye.

Another wickedly handsome face was openly grinning at her.

She shrieked and leapt off the bed, clearing the strange bodies in a single bound. Trembling against the wall, she clasped her robe and struggled into it.

"Who the hell are you? What are you doing here? How did you get in?"

Her questions ran out of steam as she got her first good look at who had been sharing her bed.

They were, in a word, splendid. A matched set, and yet different, one had a mane of hair that was so blond it was almost silver, while the other had long dark curls with glints of fire. They shared magnificent chests, broad shoulders and arms that were solid, strong and firmly muscled. Apparently, neither believed in clothing, because they were both stark naked. Their skins were golden—and Alana realized that it was not the gold of a tan, but a real golden glow—almost as if they were acting as their own light source.

Unashamed, they lay on the bed gazing at her, one resting on a propped up arm, the other with his hands casually behind his head.

She couldn't help herself—she looked...

Even at rest, they were flaunting equipment as splendid as she'd expected. Two thick, solid and well-developed cocks nestled in beds of softly curling hair, the color contrasts pleasing to the eye. Alana gazed, fascinated, as they lay there smiling, almost as if they were basking in her approval.

"Okay—did Janet put you up to this? Are you two Chippendale dancers or a strip-o-gram or something?" She pulled her robe tighter and knotted the belt securely.

"And what's with the blue fog? It might work on Halloween, but not in early September—too spooky."

One turned to the other.

"She is not aware of our identity, my brother."

"Indeed not, my brother. We should enlighten her before our tutoring duties can begin."

As one, they rose and bowed gracefully to Alana. Given her present garb, she felt it rather inappropriate to curtsy back, but it was close...

"I am Sami and this is my brother Hari. We are from the pleasure dimension and we are here to see to your education in all things pleasurable."

Sami (the blond one, mentally categorized Alana so that she could keep them straight) waved his hand around the room expansively. "You will become our student."

"I'm dead, aren't I?"

"By the gods, no, Mistress Alana. You are certainly not dead. Did you not just prove that conclusively?" said Hari in a deeply seductive voice.

Alana's buttocks clenched against the memory of her orgasm.

"In that case, I'm in a coma," she replied. "Definitely a coma. Or this is some kind of drug-induced hallucination—or...no that can't be right, because I don't do drugs. So it's a regular orgasm-induced hallucination—hey yeah, that's it..." She pressed herself even further back against the wall.

"No wait—it's that damn Blue Lotus. I could smell it earlier from that vessel..." Her voice trailed off as she looked at the vessel. There were no handles on its sides at all—it was smooth all the way around. She looked at Sami and Hari and at Sami's and Hari's cocks. She looked at the vessel again, and the cocks again.

"I'm going mad," she moaned, slithering down to the floor in a lump.

Two chuckles greeted this statement as Sami bent down and casually picked her up off the floor.

"Hey—what—just you put me...where are you taking me?" Completely befuddled by the ease with which she had been picked up off the floor—and she wasn't a lightweight stick woman, either—Alana stuttered into silence as she was carried into the bathroom.

Sami gently lowered her onto the closed toilet seat.

"Now, Mistress Alana, sit and listen while we prepare your bath."

"But I already took a shower…"

Both heads turned and gazed solemnly at her.

"Sorry."

"Sami and I are travelers. We go where we are needed to help people of this world discover the truth which lies inside them." Hari was testing the water from the faucets as he spoke, his soothing voice calming Alana's troubled spirit.

"We are from a race of beings called Djinn—what your children's tales call genies."

Alana tilted her head to one side. "As in rub the lamp and out you pop, I suppose. Well, hell. I sure did rub the lamp. Aren't I supposed to get three wishes or something?"

Sami laughed. "That is so yesterday, Mistress," he grinned, and Alana couldn't help smiling back at his huge blue eyes that definitely twinkled at her. "Today we travel throughout your world, and others known only to our kind, and we don't grant wishes so much as help you get in touch with your inner sexuality…" He gently laid a finger on her cleavage, making her body tingle.

"So you're asking me to believe that you two are some sort of intergalactic Dr. Ruth counseling service that's going to help me get in touch with my inner slut? And I do this by having wild genie sex with the both of you. Yeah, right. See this? This is my 'Oh-sure-I-buy-that' face…" Alana snorted from a combination of stress and arousal.

No getting away from it, these were two bodacious men, and they *were* naked, and they were in *her* bathroom…

"I don't think Dr. Ruth is a good analogy, my brother…" added Hari, as he stirred some sort of oil into the bath water. A wonderful fragrance rose into the steamy air and Alana felt dizzy for a second or two.

"Hey—how do you two know about Dr. Ruth anyway?" she asked suspiciously.

"She has her own show on cable."

"Wait a minute. You guys have cable in your bottle—er—vessel—er—*thing*…?" They exchanged rather embarrassed glances.

"Aha." Alana smirked at them. "I knew you two were fakes. You couldn't get cable in there…"

"Well, actually, we do get it but we don't have a legal converter," said Hari, busying himself with the bath.

"Wait—how do you…" What am I doing? I'm arguing with a pair of genies over whether they get cable TV in their bottle. I should be asking them if they get the premium services! Closing her eyes, Alana gave in to the moment.

"Yes, we do get the premium services too…" grinned Sami, watching Alana's face as she struggled to adjust to this wild situation.

"You must love the Playboy channel," she murmured, trying hard not to look at Hari's buns as he turned off the water. Ohmigod, they were so fine…

Sami straightened and faced her without his usual smile. "No, Mistress. We do not enjoy that channel. It is demeaning to women. The men are mostly unattractive and do not take care of themselves, and they can last only for a very short time. We have yet to see the act of love performed correctly."

"And the production values are very poor. It's sad…" added Hari thoughtfully.

"But enough—time to begin your learning program." Hari scooped Alana off the toilet seat and held her over the tub. Blue petals were now floating in the water and a soft, seductive fragrance curled around her legs like steam.

"My robe, wait, don't drop me."

"I would not dream of doing that, Mistress, and we must certainly rid you of that—did you call it a robe?" Sami had swiftly unknotted her bathrobe and slid it away from her body almost before she knew it had happened. He held it out to the side with a puzzled look on his face.

"Mistress, I am sorry to complain of your attire, but even the lowliest of our eunuchs would not wipe his shoes with this—this rag."

"Hey! That's my favorite bathrobe. It may not be brand new or expensive, but it is comfortable, and I love it!"

Hari sighed. "Sit, Mistress, we must brush your hair before you bathe." He urged her down onto a towel he had folded over the edge of the large bathtub, and as she sat, Sami began to brush her hair.

She couldn't help it, she closed her eyes, trying to remember the last time somebody had brushed her hair just because he wanted to. It was wonderful. Then another pair of hands smoothed her hair away from her face and gently pinned it on top of her head.

"Now, Mistress, into the water with you." She opened her eyes and gasped to see Sami standing in the tub with his hands out waiting for her to join him.

Her eyes widened and she hesitated.

"Mistress, our job is to release you from those bonds which hold the *real* you imprisoned within. To do this we will find ways to demonstrate to you what your body and your mind and your heart are capable of feeling and experiencing. Put yourself in our hands—let us help and do what we are trained to do." Hari's chocolate voice poured over Alana and she gave a mental shrug.

"What the heck. If this is a hallucination, it's a damn fine one. I'd be an idiot not to enjoy it to the max." Surprising herself, she slowly sank into the tub, relishing the warmth and the feel of the scented water as it lapped against her skin.

Sami knelt in front of her and she felt Hari settle himself outside on the floor behind her.

"Okay boys, do your worst," she said bravely.

"Oh I don't think it's our worst, by any means, just our beginning lessons," murmured Hari.

She gasped as his hands gently swished the water around her breasts. Sami had grabbed the soap and had begun to lather her toes. Why hadn't she realized her toes were so sensitive? Especially when her breasts were surfing waves made by another pair of strong hands?

Sami moved up to her calves, and Hari helped himself to another bar of soap, working up a lather that he massaged into her shoulders.

"This soap—it's not my regular soap, is it?" mumbled Alana, adrift on a sea of sensation.

"No, Mistress. We carry some necessary teaching aids with us. This is our own Blue Lotus soap, made for us by Nubians with the plant which blooms only at night along the banks of a faraway river…" Hari's voice trailed off as his hands began to make smooth, soapy circles around her breasts. Sami was continuing his journey north and had reached her thighs. It seemed as if the water was getting hotter, someone had turned the heat on, or her body was experiencing a violent thermal reaction. Okay, it was probably the latter, because she was starting to throb, warmly, not too far north of Sami.

She rested her head back and found Hari's shoulder conveniently there. His lips brushed her ear followed by a light breath of air. Her nipples puckered and Hari favored them with a soapy caress. Meanwhile, Sami was lathering her thighs and stroking the soap rhythmically along her muscles, getting nearer and nearer to her pulsating woman's flesh. She could almost feel herself swelling.

Sami eased her legs further apart so that he could sit comfortably between her thighs. Hari gently put his hands beneath her armpits and lifted her body slightly as Sami slid his long legs underneath her buttocks. She was now essentially sitting on Sami's legs.

Hari returned his attention to her breasts as Sami began tenderly soaping her tight black curls. She moaned slightly as his fingers found her clit and teased it lightly for a second or two.

"Not yet, Mistress. This is for you to enjoy and relax — do not rush. We have much ahead of us."

Thinking that if it got much better than this, she was absolutely going to expire of bliss, Alana merely sighed and moved her shoulders so that Hari could get a better grip on both breasts.

A familiar sensation brought her head up with a snap.

"What the hell do you think you're doing?"

Sami glanced up from where he was running a razor over her mound. "I am shaving you, Mistress."

"Well I can see that, you—you genie. I don't want to be shaved...do you hear? Stop that, I'll get those awful ingrown nubbies, I *hate* it." She tried to dislodge Sami by easing away from him.

Hari stilled her with his hands on her breasts, while Sami held her thighs apart with his hands.

"Mistress, I do not intend to shave you bald, but at the moment you are as hairy as a Himalayan trader."

She snorted, having no idea exactly what Himalayan traders looked like, but figuring that yaks probably had to be in there somewhere.

"Well don't you dare make a cute shape down there— no champagne glasses or lightning bolts, thank you very much."

Sami bit his lip, while Hari turned his head away, turning a laugh into a cough.

"Mistress Alana, by removing some of your hair, we will reveal skin which will be sensitive to the slightest touch. Warmth and pressure will be greater, and your sensual pleasures will multiply. Is this not a good thing? Is it not worth a few moments now and then to deal with the—what did you call them—*nubbies*?"

"Really?" she asked.

"Watch," answered Hari.

Sami delicately wielded the razor and within moments, Alana's mound was tidily trimmed down to a much smaller tuft of curls. Then Sami put his hands beneath her and raised her from the water.

"What—hey—he's..." she stuttered.

"Watch..." said Hari again, running his tongue around her ear as his fingers rolled her nipples between his soapy fingers.

Sami ran his tongue over her newly smooth flesh, and then gently blew on it.

Alana nearly went through the roof.

"Ohmigod... Ohmigod..." Incapable of speech, she watched as Sami's talented tongue took over and swirled over her mound and down toward her clit. She knew she was soaking wet. Between Hari and Sami and the soap and the bare skin she was one great big quivering, raw, exposed sex nerve and someone was about to get on it.

Hari held her close to his chest and continued to work her ears, neck and throat with his tongue. His fingers pulled and pinched and mounded her breasts as they swelled with arousal, and Sami's mouth worked her weeping pussy as she gasped for breath.

Sobbing, she tried to pull back, but Sami would not let her break their contact, gripping her buttocks hard with his strong fingers.

"Let it go, Mistress. Let it go—come for us—come now..."

"Come now, Alana—*Come*..." Hari's voice in her ear was the finishing touch, and with a scream of pleasure, Alana came. And came. And came.

Chapter Three

Morning crept into Alana's bedroom in slow degrees. The leaves that shaded her windows also admitted the dappled sunrise, and it was to this gentle light that she usually awoke. This particular morning, the light was coupled with the fragrant scent of coffee and Alana smiled and breathed deeply as she stretched her legs like a cat.

"Ooof."

"Sore, Mistress?"

Her eyes flew open and met the brilliant blue of Sami's gaze as he raised himself up and began soothing her thighs with his warm hand.

"Holy cow! You guys weren't a dream, were you?" Her head swiveled to the other side of the bed, but it was empty.

"Where's Hari?"

"Hari slept in our home. For this past night, mine was the pleasure of holding you as you slept. I believe he's making coffee for us as we speak."

Too content to fuss about who'd been cuddling whom, Alana simply nodded and relaxed into Sami's arms. His magic fingers were doing wonderful things to her sleep-warmed skin, and she could not recall feeling such physical bliss in a man's embrace— ever.

"Mmmm, Sami…" she murmured, feeling his hands caressing her mound with gentle strokes as his lips brushed across her breast. His hair was soft and fine, and teased her skin, leaving tingles of pleasure behind. He was oh-so-slowly arousing her, but definitely succeeding. She felt the telltale moisture begin to pool between her legs.

"Relax, Alana—'tis the best way to start the day," said Sami as he rubbed his strong body along hers and slid down to her pussy. His incredible tongue took over, smoothing her juices over her swollen flesh, teasing, flicking, sucking and playing in every nook and cranny he could find. His hands soothed her belly, cupped her freshly shaved mound and then worked their way back up to her nipples, rubbing, rolling and pulling them to excruciating peaks of sensitivity.

Her head arched back deep into the pillow as wave after wave of orgasmic pleasure swept her body. Her pussy seemed to clench and spasm forever, drowning his tongue as it encouraged the sensations, sweeping her from one peak to the next in a gentle frenzy.

"Wow…" she gasped, trying to catch her breath. "That was…that was something *else*."

Sami smiled, her moisture gleaming on his handsome face. Another small tremor of pleasure shook her as she gazed at this incredible man.

"You see, Alana, not every climax must make you scream and reach the stars. Some can roll gently over you…"

"Yeah—an orgasmic steamroller. You've killed me, Sami. I am now officially dead. The death certificate will say I died of extreme pleasure." Alana let her body flop onto the bed, powerless to do anything more than grin.

"I guess that means this coffee will go to waste."

She turned her head to see Hari leaning against the doorjamb with a cup of something steaming and fragrant in his hand. To judge by his arousal, he'd been watching Sami as he ate his way into Alana's record books.

Alana drooled. Okay, so maybe it was Hari rather than the coffee, but there was only so much a girl could take first thing in the morning, and Sami had already pushed her over the edge once.

"Oh. Coffee. Hmmm…Well, that's another thing altogether." Alana rolled slowly out of bed, embarrassed by the stickiness coating her thighs. "You know, hold that coffee for five minutes. I really need a quick shower." She looked firmly at them both. "Alone?"

Two grins met her gaze.

"Of course, Alana. We will prepare some food in your kitchen. Enjoy your shower."

Standing beneath the pounding water, Alana rested her hand against the shower wall and closed her eyes. What a wild night.

For someone who had previously considered herself frigid, to come so frantically with two men she'd never met before was a revelation. Yet, she was suffering no ill effects, other than a few odd twinges in muscles that hadn't been used in years.

And another thing, neither Hari nor Sami had given a thought to their own satisfaction, yet she knew they had both been aroused. Knew it? Hah. How could she miss it? Or them, rather. Thick and proud, those guys boasted cocks that could probably make the Guinness Book of World Records for beauty. There seemed to be areas of this sensuality school that hadn't been covered yet. Hmmm.

Questions flooded her mind as she soaped herself back into a state of relative un-stickiness, the scent of the lather bringing vivid memories of her erotic bath to mind.

The bubbles dribbled over her newly shaved mound, and she smiled to herself as she remembered Sami's face while he tidied her hair and then raised her aching clit to his lips. Amazingly, her nipples pebbled under the stream of warm water as she relived the feel of Hari's hands caressing her. Her body pulsed, nerve endings trembling—just the memories of that experience were turning her on.

Helplessly she slid her hands down over her breasts, cupping them and holding their soft weight in her palms. One hand slipped further, moving down past her navel to her pussy, where her juices were now mingling with the warm fragrant water.

Alana raised one leg and rested it on the side of the tub. Imitating Sami's tongue, she allowed her fingers to flick against her sensitive clit as her other hand pulled and rolled her nipples. Her buttocks clenched, and in a completely abandoned manner, she thrust two fingers into herself as the tension mounted within her and she knew she was about to come.

This was something else! She was astounded at the feel of her own spasming muscles that were pulsing around her fingers, and blown away by that sensation as much as by the orgasm she was enjoying.

Leaning against the wall, she caught her breath and allowed the shower to cool her overheated body. What was happening to her? What magic had these two Djinns performed that had turned her into a sexually obsessive woman? And should she be feeling so good about it?

Blushing, she rushed through the rest of her shower.

A remarkably tidy room greeted her. The bed was made with fresh linens, her clothes had been picked up, and that coffee was now smelling like flowers on the doorstep of heaven. Wrapped in a bath towel, she hunted for her robe.

"Dammit! What did they do with it?" She peeked under the bed, in the closet, and even checked her dresser drawers. Nothing.

She strode into the kitchen with a frown on her face. "Hey, guys. I want my robe and I want it—I want—oh, lord…"

The fire went out of her as she got her first look at Hari and Sami with clothes *on*. Either one could have modeled for Calvin Klein and tripled his profit margins within the week.

Sami had chosen a pair of jeans, which looked comfortably worn, and hugged every inch of his magnificent body. His butt cried out to be cupped by a pair of hands (hers would do quite nicely), and the denim had faded to nearly white over the crotch where a very nicely lumpy package was obviously tucked away. In a very typical male gesture, he had not fastened the top button. Why did guys do that? Did they know it turned her on?

Hari, on the other hand, had gone for leather. Not the Harley-dude leather, but the soft suede leather of a very well worn pair of pants. The shiny knees and gleaming crotch told of days spent working and playing in these clothes, and he too had omitted buttoning his last button. God, she didn't stand a chance.

Gathering her rather scattered thoughts, she yanked her towel more tightly around her and glared at her guests.

"My robe seems to have disappeared. Would either of you gentlemen happen to know where it is?" A raised eyebrow accompanied this question, and Sami and Hari turned equally innocent faces toward her.

"Robe? You would like a robe, Alana?" asked Hari, with his best butter-won't-melt-in-my-mouth look.

"Oh cut out the wide-eyed puppy bit. Yes. My robe. The one you said your eunuch wouldn't clean his windows with or something."

"Actually, there are no windows in the harem, in your sense of the word, therefore our eunuchs would not require rags to clean them," said Sami thoughtfully.

A sound that quite closely approximated the growl of a wolf about to strike down its prey emanated from Alana's throat, surprising even her.

"My robe was not a rag. It was MY robe. I loved that robe. I have watched TV in that robe, gotten drunk in that robe, been sick in that robe and spent whole sybaritic days hanging around in that robe. I have a deep sentimental attachment to that robe. Now where is it?"

The men looked at each other, guilt written in very large letters across their handsome faces. Alana was hard pressed not to smile, but bit the inside of her cheeks firmly and continued to glare angrily at them. *Let's see them squirm out of this one,* she thought.

Hari rose to pour her some coffee. "Well, Alana, it was like this...cream, sugar? Perhaps a little rosewater as well?"

"Just cream. Don't change the subject."

"I—er—it ended up near our home and I took it with me last night—and I forgot that it was trash pickup day today, and the camel sellers took everything. Including your robe." Hari looked uncomfortably down at his cup.

Alana's lips twitched. She couldn't help herself. Hari looked so apologetic, and obviously hadn't a clue that he was so gorgeous she'd forgive him just about anything.

"So that would be your third century BC version of 'the dog ate my homework'?"

Hari's eyes met hers and a twinkle started deep in their brown depths.

"I would say that is an accurate assessment, yes, Alana."

"What happened to 'Mistress,' by the way?" she added, sitting carefully at the table while trying to hold up the towel. "Not that I mind, you understand, but I was sort of getting into the 'slave/mistress' thing."

The coffee was unusual, dark yet sweet, and Alana sighed with pleasure as she replaced the mug on the table.

"Once we have brought you to your woman's pleasure a sufficient number of times, we usually dispense with the term, Alana," answered Sami from behind her. "You trust us now, and know we mean you no harm or disrespect."

She turned, realizing in a flash that he was right. She'd known them for only a few short hours, and yet she'd put her life into their hands if necessary. It was an odd moment of awareness, and she welcomed the distraction that Sami was making with a large show of producing something from behind him.

"Your robe, Alana..." he said, bowing and holding out a garment toward her.

She couldn't help it—she gasped.

It was pure white silk, such a soft and slithery silk that she could hear the folds as they brushed against each other. She carefully reached out and took it from Sami's outstretched hands. Holding it up she saw the exquisite red embroidery that circled the neck and the side slits. It was a caftan, but more luxurious and magnificent than she had ever seen.

"Oh guys..." she breathed, holding it against herself. "This is too much..."

"And also this..." Sami was holding what looked like a handful of fairy dust.

He moved his hands slightly and the sparkles turned into a finely wrought chain. A small chime came from a little bell suspended at one end.

"What's that?" she asked, fascinated by the soft sound.

"It's your *cushi* bell," said Sami, moving the chain so that the delicate ringing could be heard more clearly.

"What's a *cushi* bell?"

"Let me show you..." and Sami moved to the table and pulled Alana to her feet, incidentally leaving the bath towel on the chair behind her.

"Cushi is a Sanskrit word," began Hari, as Sami pulled her arms out to her sides and put the chain around her naked waist. "It means 'ditch' in a literal sense, but has been associated with the Greek *kunnos* and the Latin *cunnus*. So actually, this *cushi* bell is a cunt bell. Now, we are aware that your society frowns on that word, and frankly we agree that it's an ugly kind of word and sadly used for a most beautiful body part. So we prefer to call it the *cushi* bell — same meaning, better sound."

Alana watched as Sami adjusted the chain. He took his time with the teeny links, and when he was finally satisfied he stood back, motioning to Alana to walk across the room.

She took a step and froze. As she walked, the surprisingly heavy small bell swung right against her clit. Each step was an exercise in arousal.

"Dear God! I can't stand this. I'll be completely insane by the end of the day." She looked helplessly at Hari and Sami, who were smiling at her.

Hari reached over to the counter for something.

"This is all part of your beginner's classes, Alana. The function of this bell is not to bring you to orgasm every time you walk across a room, but to remind you of your own sexuality. You will see that if you walk a little more slowly and sway your hips slightly, the bell will not fall directly on your lovely clit, but just swing from side to side. The sound is also to remind you that you are a woman—bells are closely associated with everything female in our culture."

Alana tried a few more steps, following Sami's instructions. To her amazement, it worked. She turned with a smile and was suddenly blinded as Hari snapped a Polaroid of her standing there in her *cushi* bell, a big smile and absolutely nothing else. Not even mascara. She was horrified.

But Sami forestalled her before she could begin the rant she felt building up inside. "Forgive us, Alana," he said apologetically. "We take a picture of all our students—and we ask you to write your name on it too. You see—" He paused and glanced at Hari. "When we go, we will leave more than our teachings behind, we will leave our memories too. As soon as we both re-enter the vessel and seal the top, it will be for us as if we were never here. We will not remember you at all."

Chapter Four

Alana cradled her coffee mug in her hand as she sat at the table, looking at the two handsome faces across the expanse of white tile. It had taken her a few moments to grasp the significance of what Sami had told her and place it into context. She felt a wave of sadness for them sweeping over her.

"I think it's time we talked, you two," she said. "I have a lot of questions."

Hari and Sami exchanged brief glances.

"Alana, not many of our students wish to talk very much. Are you sure you would not rather work some more on your lessons?" asked Hari, a look of puzzlement on his handsome face.

"Well, this is me, and I want to talk. I need to understand some things here, and if I'm to accept that you are going to hold the future of my sex life in your hands, I think it's only fair that I get to check out your references, so to speak. Look at this as an on-the-job interview."

"Very well, Alana," agreed Hari. "What do you want to know?"

Alana narrowed her eyes slightly and fixed both of them with an unyielding stare. "How did you end up in that bottle?"

There was silence for a moment, then Sami looked at Hari. "Perhaps I will leave this story to you, my brother," he said.

Hari shrugged slightly and leaned back, the expanse of his chest a definite distraction.

"Sami and I met while campaigning in Gaul," he began.

"So you're not really brothers?"

"No. I am from a small town in what used to be Persia, while Sami is Thracian."

"Well that explains the coloring, I suppose…"

"Alana, are you going to keep interrupting or do you want to hear the story?"

"Sorry. Go on, go on…"

"Sami and I attained a somewhat dubious reputation within our phalanx. There were few women who could resist us, and we certainly took advantage of it. I make no apologies, Alana. It was a different time and we did not expect to survive the campaign. In fact, few soldiers made it home in one piece, and Sami and I were unfettered by family or loved ones. We knew that we could fight and die as free men."

Alana swallowed, struck by the stupidity of the things men could do to each other.

"We did not know at that time, but our actions were observed and reported to a kind of 'Supervisor'—one who watches for those people who possess an unusual amount of sexual skill. This man, our guide, visited us in our tent one evening and proposed that we leave our lives as soldiers and join his organization instead."

"Of course, once he told us what it was, we were convinced that we had been killed in that afternoon's fighting, and he was a messenger of the gods come to take us to the other side," added Sami, a wry twist to his lips.

"Sure enough, within moments he had us traveling with him through strange places until we ended up in Anyela — the place where we were to be trained."

"Anyela? I've never heard of it. Was it around the Mediterranean?"

Two smiles answered her question.

"Yes and no," continued Hari. "It *is* around the Mediterranean, but it's also around several other planets in different areas of this local cluster."

"Hoo boy, you're getting beyond me now. Is there a *Dimensional Travel For Dummies* version to this bit?" Alana frowned and tried to remember all those public television specials she'd dozed through.

"Just imagine that time is a bunch of ribbons, all streaming pretty much in one direction," said Sami.

"Okay. I got that."

"There are places where the ribbons become tangled and lines cross and knot, almost like a station. The ribbons come into this knot and go out again the other side, but not always on the same track."

"So you're saying that Anyela is one of these knots?"

"Anyela is actually within one of these knots — a place where time holds still, and many wise men gather to assess the progress of the universe."

"Oh my."

"And the people are very beautiful, the flowers bloom eternally, and there is no want or pain or disease," added Sami.

"It sounds like heaven," breathed Alana, trying to imagine such a place in her mind.

"It may well be what your religion describes as heaven," agreed Hari. "To us it is simply home."

"Do you have a family? Wives, kids?"

Sami looked down at the table. "Because of what we do, Alana, such things are forbidden to us. We must remain unfettered in order to love our students."

"Love your students? What does that mean?"

"It means, Alana, that each student is carefully selected for us. She must be someone whom we can love. That love is what enables us to give her the pleasure and the self-awareness she needs."

"You mean you're both going to fall in love with *me*?" squeaked Alana.

The full lips curved into identical smiles.

"We already have. Our minutes are filled with your thoughts, your scents, the feel of your skin next to our bodies…we are eagerly awaiting the moment when you are finished with this talking and we can get back to our lessons," murmured Hari, stroking her wrist with butterfly touches of his thumb.

Ignoring the chills running up and down her spine, Alana doggedly continued. "Back up the truck there, buster. I have plenty more questions yet."

Hari sighed. Sami rolled his eyes.

"Cut that out, both of you. A few more minutes won't hurt." Alana couldn't help but wonder if any of their students had taken the time to get to know them before now.

"Don't you ever wish you could settle down? Have a family? Age normally?"

Silence fell for a moment as both men considered her words.

Sami was the first to answer. "I suppose if we were given the choice, we might elect to stay in one place with...with one woman, but because we never remember our last student, it would be pretty much impossible for us."

Alana was beginning to get a picture and wasn't too sure if she liked what she saw.

"So—let me get this straight. You two have been traveling through time, being assigned to women with whom you can't help falling in love. How is that calculated, by the way?"

"Something to do with pheromones and their DNA constituents, I believe," answered Sami.

Hari raised an eyebrow and looked at him. "Did the Guardian tell you that?"

Sami colored slightly. "Nope. Saw a special on The Learning Channel."

"Hah."

"Excuse me. Save the squabbles, I'm pursuing a train of thought here. After fulfilling your mission of awakening her sexual identity, you two blast off into the ether and have no memories of her—just arriving back at home with a suitcase full of dirty laundry and a photograph? No recollection of the love you've shared or anything she's said and done?"

"As long as our mission has been successfully completed, that is correct. And we've not had an unsuccessful mission yet, have we Sami?"

"No, never. We are, in fact, the best at what we do." Sami said this with pride, not boastfulness, and Alana couldn't help but smile.

"I can certainly vouch for that," she answered.

Two pairs of eyes lit up and the sexual tension in the room ratcheted up ten notches.

"Wait…" she held up a hand, palm outward. "I'm not quite finished."

Two groans answered her.

"First, I'd like to know who does what in this arrangement. So far it's been mostly Sami—not that I'm complaining, but I'd like to know the curriculum, so to speak, and secondly…" She cleared her throat and swallowed, trying to find the words for her next question. "Why haven't either of you come yet? And inside me? Is that not allowed? Or can't you…"

Hari's hand slammed down on the table, making Alana jump. "Oh we can, Alana, never doubt that. I'm surprised you could even think that we couldn't."

"Okay! Geez, I'm sorry. That wasn't a slur on your masculinity. Some things obviously never change. I'm dealing with a lot of unknowns here, guys. You're going to have to cut me a little slack. Seeing as we are letting it all hang out, so to speak, I have one more question. Can you get me pregnant? Are we supposed to use genie Trojans?"

Hari looked at Alana, an almost wistful expression on his face. "That is not a problem, Alana. We do not have the capability of reproducing."

"But you certainly have the equipment. Have you had your tubes snipped—are you on some kind of pill, what?"

Both men had grimaced and crossed their legs at her questions. A gleam came into Sami's eyes.

"Perhaps we should demonstrate for you, Alana. Would you permit that?"

"Um...sure, I guess. What does it involve?"

"The bed."

"How did I guess that?"

"And Hari and I," continued Sami. "With you seated before us. May we show you?"

He took her hand and led her into the bedroom, where he carefully smoothed back the covers of the freshly made bed. He waved his hand, Hari muttered a few words of a strange language and their clothes disappeared. *All* their clothes, including her lovely caftan. The bell had stayed put.

"Hey! What the—"

"Do not be concerned, Alana, it is a simple party trick of ours. It saves time too, come to think of it. You shall have your robe returned to you shortly. In the meantime, enjoy the feel of the air against your body. Celebrate the freedom of being unclad with us."

Closing her eyes for a moment, Alana tried to stop worrying about her slightly rounded stomach, the scar on her upper thigh and whether or not her buttocks looked lumpy. Celebrate freedom, indeed. Obviously these guys didn't read *Vogue* magazine.

These worries, however, were wiped from her brain as she settled herself against the footboard amidst the covers and watched as Hari and Sami lay down next to each other with a warm smile. The affection they felt for each other was in their eyes at that moment and brought a lump to Alana's throat, then a gasp as they reached down and firmly grabbed the other's cock.

* * * * *

Alana sat, mouth agape, as the two began to gently slide their hands up and around their semi-erect cocks. Within moments she realized that she could probably drop the word "semi" from her vocabulary.

Never in a million years had she dreamed that she would actually sit on her bed and watch while two gorgeous hunks of steamy, masculine sex-appeal brought each other satisfaction — with nothing but their hands.

Fascinated, she inched closer, eyes trapped on the spectacle of two firm male hands slithering up and down and around two engorged cocks. Glancing up she saw that Sami's eyes had closed, while Hari's had narrowed to two slits as their hands gripped tighter and moved faster.

"Come closer, Alana. Don't be afraid," whispered Hari, noting her close scrutiny. "Yes. Join us Alana — come and share. Giving pleasure to another is one of the universe's greatest joys," encouraged Sami.

Unable to resist, Alana inched up the bed until she was kneeling between them. They turned their bodies slightly away from each other so that she could have a better view. She gulped.

The sound of slick flesh rhythmically sliding over slicker flesh was hypnotic, and Alana found herself panting with arousal.

Sami moved toward her, interrupting his rubbing for a moment to pass his hand across the moisture that was welling from her body. He returned to Hari's cock and smeared her juices over its length, paying special attention to the ridge and the underside.

Hari moaned in pleasure and slanted a quick look and a nod at Alana, indicating that she should do the same for Sami.

"Well, nothing ventured," she muttered, and following Hari's subtle message, she passed her hand between her thighs and bent to attend to Sami.

Imitating Hari's motions as best she could, she began to smooth the length of Sami's cock, as Hari gently removed his hand and let her take over. He covered her hand with his and showed her how firmly to grip Sami, and how to run her fingers around and across the sensitive opening at the tip. Sami's were the groans that now filled the air.

Satisfied that she had understood the basic principles, Hari moved a little and reached for Alana's clit. Thinking he simply meant to gather more of her juices, she widened her stance slightly to give him access. Nothing prepared her for the sharp upward thrust of two solid fingers.

Gasping, she clamped onto Sami's cock eliciting a similar gasp from him.

"Oh God, Sami—I'm sorry, did I hurt you?" she croaked.

"Only if you stop now..." hissed Sami through clenched teeth.

Hari's hands worked Alana with the same rhythm she was using on Sami and Sami was using on Hari—the whole room seemed to be vibrating in time with their movements, and Alana's *cushi* bell was ringing furiously.

Within moments Alana felt the first ticklings of an orgasm, and her muscles clenched. She noted absently that Sami's hand was working Hari faster, and she tried to copy his rhythm, even though she was distracted by Hari's fingers pumping into her pussy.

Apparently, everyone was nearing the peak of their pleasure, because Hari suddenly rubbed Alana's clit hard with his thumb, and she shrieked as her orgasm hit. Shivering and shaking, and still on her knees, she rolled through the spasms with teeth gritted, hanging onto Sami's cock for dear life.

She came down slowly, aware that the two men were simmering on the edge of orgasm—their cocks now fully extended and very swollen, and their balls tight to their bodies. Watching her climax was clearly adding to their arousal.

Obeying an instinct, Alana bent to where the two bodies were so close and quickly ran her tongue up the underside of first Hari's and then Sami's cock. She carefully put her hands beneath their balls and cradled them, rolling them around in her hands.

They quickly grabbed each other's cock and with a few strong, intense strokes, Alana could see their climax begin.

Bodies arching, teeth clenching, they pulled away slightly—buttocks thrusting each cock into the other's hands. With a loud moan, they came.

Alana's jaw dropped.

Instead of the copious amounts of creamy cum she'd anticipated, clouds of blue vapor were belching out from the slits at the tips of their cocks.

It was scented slightly with the fragrance of Blue Lotus and glistened where the sunlight bounced off it. It was like a mixture of blue fog and fairy dust. And it had been all over her that first night.

Chapter Five

Alana looked at the bodies sprawled across her on the rumpled bed. She smiled at the sight of Hari, head resting on her belly, breath whiffling her mound and hand firmly holding her inner thigh.

Sami had cuddled under her arm, using her breast as a convenient pillow — his lips so close to her nipple that he could have suckled it without moving an inch. His arm lay heavily under her breasts, holding her to him even in sleep.

A warm wave of affection swamped her, and tears rose into the back of her eyes. She wondered at these two amazing beings who, within twenty-four hours, had become practically her entire life.

Of course that hadn't been too hard. She leaned her head back comfortably on the pillow and gazed at the few little glistening particles that dotted her ceiling.

It was Labor Day weekend, so she had no reason to hurry anywhere. The store would be closed for the holiday, and she had her customary week's vacation planned. Labor Day marked the end of the tourist season, and her business always slowed to a trickle for this month. It was a good time for inventory and traveling to estate sales, picking up merchandise that would sell well in the upcoming holiday season.

Other than Janet, her friends were busy with their own lives. Most were married, and it got harder to keep up a regular kind of friendship when one person became part of a couple and the other didn't. Oh, they were all still there, but their lives were taking different paths. Alana wasn't sure if she wanted to go down that path or not.

However, Sami and Hari had certainly begun to teach her that she could be a very sexual creature—something she'd never have guessed about herself. Sex, up until now, had been pleasant occasionally, messy most of the time, and once or twice, damned uncomfortable. There was My-Big-Mistake-George who thought that a quick kiss and the fact that he was her neighbor entitled him to bang her up against her own kitchen counter. Then there was Mr-Let's-Be-Wild-and-Do-It-In-My-Car Michael, who never added that he drove a Honda Civic. It had taken her four visits to the chiropractor to straighten out the kinks. Not to mention that Michael wanted to be wild on wheels because his apartment contained his fiancée, who might have been quite upset at the whole idea.

Alana grimaced at herself. She'd sure fucked up when it came to fucking!

Until now.

Comfortably snuggled between two of the sexiest men this side of—of—well, there weren't any comparisons, really. She had two incredible, naked men in her bed, and they were devoting themselves to making her feel like a woman. Hah. If she felt any more like a woman, she was going to drown in estrogen.

A deep feeling of gratitude swelled inside Alana, and she gazed thoughtfully at the two heads tucked onto her body. What could she do for them? Oh sure, sexual things were a given, but there must be something that two genies might like. What do you give a Djinn who has everything?

God, and she used to think buying Christmas gifts for her mother was a problem.

It probably wouldn't have been a problem if her mother hadn't critically examined each and every gift and, more often than not, returned or exchanged it. She'd given up a few years ago when her mother had announced she was moving to Florida. Proud of herself for not allowing the consequent whininess to persuade her to follow, Alana now restricted herself to the occasional phone call, cards when appropriate, and quietly relished the non-judgmental life she was now enjoying.

All of which may have contributed to her lack of interest in things sexual, but didn't suggest anything to solve her immediate problem—what she could do to say "thanks" to Sami and Hari.

Then an idea hit her, and a grin crossed her face.

Easing herself from their tangled limbs ever so slowly, she crept quietly from the room and left them sleeping soundly next to each other like exhausted puppies.

* * * * *

It was another hour before the two yawning genies struggled back to consciousness, and fifteen minutes more before they emerged from the bedroom. They were dressed—well, as much as they usually were, undone buttons and all—and they gave Alana matching embarrassed grins.

"I think that is a first," said Hari as he moved behind Alana and kissed her cheek.

"I don't ever remember napping like that before. Of course I may have, but it feels strange," added Sami with a puzzled smile.

"Something smells good. What are you making?"

Alana turned and surveyed her guests.

"Okay boys, you've been working very hard for the last few hours—probably the last few centuries—and you're clearly pooped, or you wouldn't have napped like that. So I'm declaring a sex moratorium for the rest of the day."

"Can she do that?"

"I don't know—and how can we check?"

"You don't need to check with anyone. It's a done deal. I'd have liked to take you out with me, but something tells me that might not work."

"You are right, Alana. We must stay within a certain distance of our bottle, or we become reduced to our essence and are pulled back into it."

"Hmmm... Well, I can live with that, I suppose. Oh, another question. How do I explain you if my friend Janet drops by? She's never going to buy some story about plumbing or utilities."

Hari and Sami raised their eyebrows scornfully.

"We are not service people, Alana," said Sami, a little miffed. "We have many centuries of experience behind us. You would never be able to pass us off as some kind of menial employee."

"Sorry—of course, I forgot myself there for a moment. Okay—touchy point..."

"Besides," added Hari, "Others cannot see us. We are for you only, and only you can see our presence or feel our touch. For anyone else we do not exist."

Alana mulled that one over for a moment then turned back to her task.

"Well, whatever. Now, you guys are going to experience a real twenty-first century weekend treat."

Hari grinned, and Sami started to remove his jeans.

"No—clothes on for this one, fellas. Follow me."

Pouting slightly, Sami followed Alana into her comfortable living room. She had arranged the couch directly in front of the TV and there was a low coffee table between the two. She gestured to the couch.

"Please sit, get comfortable." She padded back into the kitchen, her little bell tinkling quietly inside the sweats she'd thrown on earlier.

It had started raining a while ago, and the gloom of the afternoon was lightened by the lamps Alana had turned on around the room. Hari looked at Sami and raised his eyebrows.

"Don't ask me. I haven't a clue," Sami answered.

Alana came back into the room with an enormous bowl of something steaming and fragrant on a tray with some other little bottles next to it.

"Popcorn, guys. And a movie…" She waved the remote in the air.

"Popcorn?"

"This is corn?"

"You haven't tried it, have you?" asked Alana nervously. "I wanted to fix you something you'd never had, and I figured this might be a good start."

Sami had picked up a kernel and was holding it cautiously between thumb and forefinger. "What do we do with it?" he asked Alana.

"You eat it, sweetie...and you can sprinkle things on it. Here..." She took the little bottles off the tray one by one.

"Here's hot pepper, garlic salt, chili powder, regular salt and salt-free sprinkles. Help yourself."

To say that Hari and Sami were impressed with the popcorn would have been an understatement. Within an amazingly short time the bowl was empty—both having professed a partiality to the spicy combination of chili powder and garlic salt.

"Now for the next phase," laughed Alana, reappearing with a cold beer in each hand.

"Aha—now this we have seen on TV," grinned Hari, popping the top like a pro.

"Perfect, Alana...just perfect," sighed Sami, putting his feet up on the coffee table and leaning back with a smile of contentment.

"Oh, we're not done yet," she laughed.

Within minutes a large tray of hot buffalo wings replaced the empty popcorn bowl. It was accompanied by fresh onion dip, cone shaped crackers and an assortment of pretzels, chips and cheesy nibbles.

When everything was settled, she stepped over the coffee table in front of Hari and Sami and wiggled her bottom onto the couch between them.

"Now we can really enjoy the afternoon together," she said, grabbing the remote and searching for her movie schedule.

"Ah—would this be *Vixen Virgins* by any chance? We liked that one..."

"Or maybe *Dilys' Dildo*?"

"Guys—no sex this afternoon, remember my rule." She bit her lip as she hit "Play" and watched their faces as *Aladdin* filled the screen.

They seemed unsure when the Genie first appeared on the screen, but within moments the funny cartoon character had them holding their stomachs and rolling with laughter.

Tears trickled down Sami's face as he howled at some of the Genie's antics, and Alana felt amazingly happy that she had been able to offer them this little respite from their duties. The food disappeared, the movie ended, several more crumpled beer cans joined their mates on the coffee table, and Alana found herself surrounded by two contented bodies with cheesy fingers and garlic breath as they channel surfed around the sports networks.

"Oooh—NASCAR," Sami pointed at the screen.

Hari belched quietly. "Heavens, I'm messy. My fingers are yellow." He stared at them with fascination.

Sami snickered. "Should have stuck to the hot wings there, Har, see?" And he held out clean hands, which he had spent quite some time licking clean of barbecue sauce.

"Alana, this has been a real pleasure for us," said Hari, turning to her with a huge smile. "We will be forever in your debt."

"Even if we can't remember it," added Sami.

A quick twist of pain caught Alana around the heart. Oh well, at least they were happy at this moment.

"We must shower off this cheesy stuff though, before moving to tonight's lessons," Hari said thoughtfully, staring at the empty bowl of cheesy puffs. "I wouldn't want to get your delightful pussy all cheesy and yellow."

Alana couldn't help an anticipatory shiver as she absorbed his words. She cleared her throat. "So what's next on the schedule?"

"Tonight, Sami will continue your sensual class. I will be participating also as we will soon be moving to experiences that will mark your emergence as a truly fulfilled woman," murmured Hari.

"Oh! And we're going to do this, how?"

Sami smiled. "Never fear, Alana, we will guide you safely. But one moment, please. A good and courteous guest never leaves a mess for his hostess." With a wave of his hands and a few words, the living room became clean once again, and the empties magically appeared in Alana's recycling bin.

Awed, she looked around the room. "Can you teach me to do that?"

Both men turned to Alana and she could see the lights dancing in their eyes. "Maybe not that, but so much more, Alana, so much more."

With no prompting or touching, she knew she was in for another wild ride. A little voice inside her head whispered, "Oh goody!"

Chapter Six

"If you will permit me a few moments, Alana, I must fetch my supplies. Please allow Hari to make you comfortable while you wait."

"Supplies?" asked Alana.

"Come, Alana…all will be revealed shortly. Let me show you what I need you to do this evening."

"Bet it involves getting naked first," she muttered, keeping her fingers tightly crossed.

Following Hari into the bedroom, she watched as he rolled back the covers and arranged the pillows high on the headboard.

"This is where you will be seated for some of this evening, Alana. Would you care to make yourself comfortable?"

He waved his hands and her clothes disappeared.

"Those were my good sweats, Hari. I'll thank you not to let the camel seller take them with your trash tomorrow…" Her eyes narrowed and she stared at him.

Hari had the grace to blush slightly. "I have simply transferred them to your hamper, Alana. And your *cushi* bell is on the night table."

Looking down, Alana rubbed her hand over her stomach, feeling strangely naked without the tiny chain and her tinkling companion.

Hari helped her settle into the pillows and she reclined slightly, as comfortable and relaxed as could be for someone who was eagerly anticipating having more and better orgasms with two adorable and handsome genies. Yeah, sure she was relaxed.

The tension built as Hari left her to return to his vessel. He shimmered blue and—poof--he was gone.

Sami reappeared beside the bed holding a large bundle, which he placed on the floor.

Curious, Alana leaned over, but was blocked by Sami's body. Not a real hardship, she thought, seeing those wonderful rippling abs leading to his cute insy navel and beyond. Aaaah...beyond.

"Alana...Alana, sit up please," Hari's voice recalled her attention away from Sami's oh-so-fine cock, and she quickly sat up with a blush, realizing that Hari had taken his promised shower. His hair gleamed with moisture and was slicked back behind his ears. God, he looked scrumptious!

"Sorry! I just wanted to see what Sami brought." Besides that wonderful dream tool sticking out of his crotch, that is.

Sami grinned. "Not yet, that would spoil things." He reached down and brought a length of crimson cord onto the bed. About ten feet long with enormous tassels at each end, Alana looked at it warily.

"You're not going to whip me with that thing, are you?"

"My goodness, Alana, bondage is one of our more advanced classes. You're nowhere near ready for that yet..." said Sami, slightly shocked.

"All we are going to do is give you these tassels to hold—like so—"

He tossed one end of the cord to Hari and they both lowered the bulk of the crimson silk behind the headboard, bringing the tassels around in front and putting them into Alana's hands. To hold them, she had to stretch her arms out to either side.

"We ask that you keep holding these throughout tonight's class. We are going to concentrate on your sense of touch—your skin—and we find that if your hands are not involved, the sensitivity of your body is greatly heightened," explained Sami.

"You may, of course, release the cord at any time, but we encourage you not to— you will receive far more benefit from our exercises if you keep your hands away," added Hari.

Blowing a breath of air between her lips, Alana nodded. "I'll do my best, guys, but remember, I'm only human." Anticipation was coursing through her veins like hot lava.

Sami reached down again and stood up, this time holding something glittering in his hands. Spreading it out, he said "This is your jewelry for this evening—I regret that I must ask for its return when we are done."

Alana released a tassel and placed a finger delicately on the necklace.

"My God, I've never seen anything so beautiful…" she breathed, stroking her hand over the beads which had been interwoven into a collar.

"It was old when it came to us," smiled Hari. "We can only guess as to its history —but the style was also very popular in Egypt—I believe today you have seen similar collars in your museums, yes?"

With muddled thoughts of Tutankhamen, and Elizabeth Taylor as Cleopatra galloping through her mind, Alana gulped as Sami reached behind her head and fastened the collar. The ancient glass beads were cool and smooth against her flushed skin, and she realized that the intricate design was resting on top of her nipples. Each breath she took stirred the long beads that dripped heavily from the edge of the necklace and caressed her breasts. Oh heavens.

"No wonder Cleo was hot for *both* Caesar and Antony," she laughed, feeling the tingle her movements caused from her nipples to her pussy. So distracted was she that she failed to notice the other item Sami was now straightening in his palms.

"And lastly…" he said, bending toward her, "the most important part of this evening's experience—the blindfold."

"Oh God…Sami—do I have to?" She looked at him with a combination of fear and arousal.

"Do you trust us, Alana? Have we not proved to you that we are here only to bring you pleasure?"

It was clearly her decision, and Alana gnawed her lip, her eyes going from Sami to Hari and back. Did she trust them enough? She shouldn't—they were bizarre beings from another dimension, if what they said was true, and she'd known them for such a short time.

But something in her heart said "yes"—and she remembered the look on their faces when they talked of their lives, and ate their popcorn, and pleasured each other in front of her.

Taking a deep breath, she nodded. "I trust you both. I'm probably nuts, and I'm still thinking that maybe this is one awesome hallucination, and I'm going to wake up in some asylum somewhere covered in drool, but I trust you. Go ahead."

Sami gently covered her eyes with a scarf of the softest silk. It clung to her eyebrows and brushed the top of her cheeks—she was quite blind, not even light could penetrate the tightly woven folds. Sami carefully adjusted the fit, making sure her hair wasn't caught anywhere. His attention reassured Alana—after all, a serial killer probably wouldn't worry if her hair was tangled.

His hands moved away and she felt the loss.

"Alana," said Hari quietly. "We will be touching you and asking you to focus on what we are doing. In this exercise, what we say is often as important as what we do. Are you with us so far?"

Alana nodded, and her necklace rippled, teasing her nipples. She sucked in her breath.

She felt the bed dip as Hari clambered up, followed by a matching movement on the other side. Sami.

A hand picked up her foot, and a pair of lips brushed across her instep. Another hand took her second foot—a tongue swished over her toes and she giggled.

"Alana, you have the most beautiful feet…" murmured Hari, who she could tell was the toe-licker. "I worship them with my tongue." He matched words to action by sucking her little toe into his mouth and swirling his tongue around it.

Alana gasped a little, feeling each movement of his warm and inviting mouth send shivers to her pussy, which was beginning to show its approval of what Hari was doing by getting quite hot and wet.

Sami continued his kisses, feather-light around her foot, then stopped, moving her foot to rest on his body.

"Alana, I have placed your foot on my body. Can you tell me where?"

Alana thought for a second and wiggled her toes.

"On your chest?"

"Very good."

Hari's suckling tongue had moved to her next toe, and he was stroking the valley between them with long, sensual laps.

"Where is your foot now, Alana?" asked Sami, distracting her again.

"I—wait a minute—" Trying to shut off the sensory input from Hari and concentrate on her other foot was getting harder.

"It's—um...I can't be sure. Oh! I feel your beard. Is it on your neck?"

"Good girl."

Hari began to accompany his licking with a gentle running of his hands up and down her calf.

"Where is your foot now, Alana?" Sami asked again.

"At this point, I don't even know if it's still on the end of my leg, for heaven's sake! How can I tell when Hari is distracting me?" she grunted in response to a particularly strong tug of Hari's tongue.

"You must focus, Alana. Allow your senses to embrace whatever information they are receiving. Let each part of your skin be receptive and open your mind to the images your body is sending. We are deliberately flooding you with information—you have the skill to sort it out—now focus…" said Sami, moving her foot yet again.

She tried to obey. Relaxing the muscles in her shoulders, she grasped the tassels firmly and let her mind flood with sensation. The texture of Hari's tongue, rough in some places, smooth in others. The feel of Sami's hand beneath her heel as he held her foot against his body.

Alana found, to her amazement, that she could indeed experience both pleasures without losing her mind.

"My foot is against your upper arm, Sami. I can just barely feel that large vein that crosses your muscle there," she murmured, amazed at herself.

"And now?"

She smiled. "Dead giveaway, Sami. No matter what Hari's doing, I know that's your cock."

She heard Sami's gentle laugh, echoed by Hari.

"She is doing far too well at this, my brother," said Hari. "Let's really challenge her…"

Alana chuckled, then gasped as someone, Hari she supposed, brushed her breasts and did something to the beads at the bottom of her necklace. Now it was holding her breasts up—almost like some kind of ancient beaded bra, but the beads had started pressing into and rolling across her nipples. It was no longer a caress, but a definitely erotic arousal.

"Oh boy," she groaned, knowing that it would only get worse if she moved too much. Her hands gripped the tassels even tighter.

"Where is your foot now, Alana?" asked Sami.

She flexed her foot and wiggled her toes, but could feel nothing but firm flesh.

"Um—I need a clue," she confessed, seriously distracted by the amazingly sensual treatment her nipples were undergoing.

"Very well," said Sami, moving her foot a little.

She felt the flesh dip slightly beneath her sole then rise again.

"My God," she breathed. "That is Hari's butt. My foot is on those gorgeous buns."

"Excellent, Alana," laughed Hari. "See how sensual your feet can be?"

"Mmmm," she murmured, thoroughly enjoying exploring the two bodacious buttocks with her toes. When she slid into the crevice, however, Sami moved her foot again.

"Now we move on, Alana," he said, ignoring her little pout of disappointment.

"Would you release the tassels, please, turn over onto your stomach, and then take the tassels back into your hands?"

Alana obeyed as Sami moved the pillows to settle her comfortably. Or as comfortably as he could, given that she was lying on glass beads that were probably several thousand years old, and were at that moment digging into her nipples.

"Ignore the beads, Alana. As we progress your breasts will become even more sensitive and the necklace will become a mix of pleasure and pain. This is all part of the experience."

"Oh. Okay," she mumbled, privately wondering how long it was going to take before the potholes in her chest would fade.

There was silence for a moment, and Alana felt strangely bereft. Then the bed moved slightly, and a warm tongue stroked the length of her leg from heel to buttock.

She yelped with pleasure.

Another warm stroke caressed her thighs, and then she felt the slightest brush of something at the base of her spine.

She sucked in a breath and waited.

There—it came again—just the merest breath, but there was something touching her. Being unable to use her eyes, Alana was becoming more and more dependent on her other senses. She could hear and feel the movements of both Hari and Sami as they bent to her body.

"What's that?" she whispered, trying to hear something that would give her a clue.

"You tell me..." answered Sami.

"Don't forget to use *all* your senses, Alana," added Hari.

The sensation came again, and Alana tried to concentrate. She was certainly using her sense of touch—it was this that was driving her nuts. What else could she try? She was listening intently, and nothing helped. There was no way to taste anything. So that left smell.

She drew in a breath through her nose and there it was. The faintest touch of Blue Lotus—but sweeter somehow.

"I smell it," she grinned triumphantly.

"I smell Blue Lotus, but it's different...kind of sweeter or tangy. I can't quite tell..."

"Excellent," said Sami.

"It is indeed our Blue Lotus," said Hari, "but this is in a powdered form, and mixed with honey. That way," a light touch flickered over her buttocks, "we can dust your beautiful skin with our golden blue powder and then…"

She gasped as two tongues started firmly licking her buttocks, stroking up and down and tugging the sensitive skin of her cheeks.

"Oh. My. God." She moaned.

"A double taste treat. Our powdered delight, and your lovely essence."

Alana was helpless to respond. She lay boneless with ecstasy as two warm and fleshy tongues swirled, smoothed and licked their way around her buttocks like starving men attacking a banana split. Every touch of the powder was followed by a hungry tongue lapping it from her skin.

Her clit throbbed and she could feel her juices soaking the linens beneath her. This was the most arousing thing she could ever remember — since, well, since the last time Sami and Hari had done things to her.

She felt the pull on her cheeks getting stronger and the dust of the powder against her most intimate crevice.

"Uh guys…" she said, fighting the urge to clench her gluteal muscles lest she should catch a wayward tongue.

"Alana — trust us. Your flesh is filled with sensitive nerve endings. We are merely awakening those which have not been explored before. This is a treasure trove of pleasure points…relax…let me show you," breathed Hari.

Gnawing on her lower lip, Alana tried her best to relax. It wasn't her greatest success, but Hari obviously approved, giving a murmur of approval as he spread her cheeks once again. Sami ran his tongue up her spine and distracted her.

The gentle dust of powder settled on the puckered skin around her anus and was followed by Hari's tongue.

Alana exploded.

Chapter Seven

With a huge moan she expelled the breath she had held since she'd felt the powder dusting her delicate tissues. Every nerve ending she possessed was clapping its hands to its head and running round in circles screaming. Her nipples were as hard as the beads that were pushing against them, and her whole mound was pulsating. She didn't know whether she was coming or having a heart attack.

She tried to turn her head and speak, but realized that she'd grabbed the pillow with her teeth. She spat it out and panted.

"Easy, sweet delight," soothed Sami, dropping little butterfly kisses across her shoulders. "It's a new sensation—just relax and enjoy it."

If Alana had had the strength she would have pointed out that trying to relax, while an intergalactic genie was kissing one's ass and one's nipples were being tormented by beads the size of boulders, was probably not something she was going to be very successful at.

Hari gently moved away from her buttocks, rubbing them slowly and soothingly. Unable to help herself, Alana sighed—relieved but bereft.

She felt Sami bend to her neck and release the catch on the necklace. Hari, on the other hand, was still kissing and nipping her buttocks, keeping her arousal simmering. Gently, Sami eased the necklace out from under her chest.

The softness of the sheets was a balm to her tender breasts — although they were still extraordinarily sensitive to the slightest movement of the fabric across their tips.

"Sami — the kiss of the camel, please?" asked Hari politely.

Alana's mind blanked.

Something cool and smooth settled at the base of her spine.

"This is one of our students' favorite treats, Alana," said Sami. "I believe you will find it most pleasurable..."

She tensed as she felt a rope of beads, as smooth and as round as marbles, rolling around on her back. Hari's hand held one end to her spine and passed the other down along her cleft, letting the excess dangle across her swollen labia in a cool cascade. She sighed at the soothing feeling of the beads against her hot flesh.

Then Hari eased her cheeks apart and pulled the beads taut.

"Woweee..." she sputtered.

The beads were the perfect shape to fit snugly over her tight little anus, and when Hari increased the tension they fit her like a cork. Her tight ring of muscles was eased apart ever so slightly by the marble, and the feeling was incredible.

Her body once again registered this unfamiliar sensation by zinging her with the sexual equivalent of about a gigawatt of electric shocks.

"Alana, please release the tassels for a moment. We wish you to turn onto your back..." Sami pushed on her shoulder gently, indicating the way she was to turn.

It took almost all of her concentration to let go of the tassels. She'd become so used to hanging onto them for dear life that it was very hard to unclench her fingers.

Hari kept his hands on the beads as she gingerly rolled over, making sure that the tension never varied. He slid a little pillow beneath her back as she moved, catching the top of the beaded rope and allowing Alana's weight to hold it in place. The beads were firmly pressed against her—oh, God, were they firmly pressed against her! She couldn't decide if it was a good pressure or a bad pressure. It might take at least a couple of months for her to decide.

Her chest, however, was very relieved to be rid of its necklace, and—even better— Sami was pouring a delicately scented lotion onto her skin and beginning a soothing massage. She breathed a sigh of relief as Hari removed her blindfold and she could watch the erotic sight of Sami tending carefully to her chest.

His hands passed over and around her breasts, gentling away the dimples left by the necklace. Staying away from her nipples for the moment, he let his hands love her flesh, lifting, moving, stroking and smoothing her skin into a gentle hum.

Hari occasionally tugged slightly on the beads, just to remind her that they were there. This, thought Alana, had to be pretty close to Nirvana.

Hari brought a large pot to her side and removed a brush, which sparkled in the dim light. Alana also noticed the candles that had been lit—something she'd missed before.

The brush was as soft as a feather and Alana recognized the scent of the powder. Hari tickled the brush over her mound.

"Aaaah…" she giggled. "That tickles, Hari."

Smiling, Hari licked at the powder. "It's supposed to."

"The brush is made of camel's hair," added Sami. "We understand its softness is much prized amongst your painters."

"Not to mention make up artists," mumbled Alana, thinking of the enormously expensive brush she'd wanted for her eye shadow.

"And the 'Kiss of the Camel'?" she asked, flexing her buttocks and wincing slightly as the beads reminded her that they were still there.

"A little something to heighten the body's response to stimuli, Alana," said Hari. "Like this…" and he ran his tongue roughly over her clit at the identical moment Sami tweaked her tender nipples.

"Oh God. Choreography. I can't stand it…" she groaned.

"Yes you can, Alana. Your limits are about to be expanded," laughed Sami.

And both Hari and Sami worked together to bring her to the peak, and then soothe her down with loving caresses. They touched her with skill and affection, always stopping short of the final moment of orgasm.

What seemed like hours later, Alana felt the tears coming to her eyes.

"It's no use — either make me come or kill me, I *cannot* go on…" her voice croaked. Each of her muscles was threatening to cramp, her pussy was drowning in its own juices and her clit was getting tired of trying to attract someone's attention.

"Perhaps it is indeed time for our mid-term exam..." whispered Sami.

"Oh God, please, yes...whatever it is, just make this ache go away..." she moaned.

Hari and Sami eased her down the bed until she was quite flat, and with a kind of regret she felt the beads being withdrawn from her ass.

The mattress dipped as Hari lay down beside her and turned her onto her shoulder. He snuggled himself tight against her and pulled her buttocks into his groin.

Sami also lay on the bed, but reversed his position, putting his head down by Alana's pussy and easing his thigh under her head. She looked his cock straight in the eye.

Hari's arm eased beneath her and came up to clasp her breast, and Sami raised her leg, bending it at the knee and pushing it back slightly, exposing her completely to his sight.

Impossibly, the sexual tension in her body re-established itself and in a flash she was wet, hot and swollen. Hari's clever fingers toyed with a nipple, and his hand slid over her buttocks to her cleft. Sami moved closer—she could feel his breath on her pussy.

As one, they touched her.

The second Hari's questing finger found her puckered little hole, Sami's tongue lapped along her labia and swiped across her clit.

"Ohmigod..." she breathed.

Sami's tongue continued its exploration of her hot and weeping pussy while Hari, talented Hari, pulled and teased her nipples and gently caressed her anus.

Needing to move, Alana reached out and grabbed the nearest thing to her, which happened to be Sami's cock.

He gasped, interrupting his rhythm slightly, then went back to what he was doing.

"Gently, Alana..." reminded Hari, nipping her shoulders gently and then licking the skin. "If you wish to work Sami's cock, you may, but we do not encourage you to suck him yet...we have not trained you in this art."

Hari was truly a man of great focus, thought Alana, as she stroked her hand lovingly up and down Sami's cock.

He could nibble on her neck, fondle her breasts and circle her most delicate tissue with his finger all at the same time. She must remind herself to ask him if he could do the rub-stomach pat-head thing. She giggled a little hysterically.

"What amuses you, dear delight?" Hari's voice caressed her ear, adding another shiver to the mix.

Alana shook her head, unable to answer as Sami's tongue had just hit pay dirt.

Stepping up his rhythm, Sami was now teasing and flicking her clit—sometimes close, sometimes not close enough.

She moaned and kept her hands moving on his cock.

Sami moved closer and eased his tongue deep into her channel.

She gasped at the feeling—so warm and slick inside her. The stubble on his lightly bearded chin was doing fantastic things to the rest of her pussy. She couldn't help another moan of pleasure.

She was getting tenser and tenser now—surely Hari could feel the muscles in her buttocks trembling. His cock was wedged between them, and she tried moving very slightly on him. Sami picked up her rhythm and stayed with her, backing his tongue up to her super-sensitive clit.

Panting, she held his cock and noticed a drop of glittering blue moisture beading the tip. Obeying an irresistible urge, she moved her head and took him into her mouth.

As she did, the pressure from Hari's finger increased ever so slightly, and with a little popping sensation, he had suddenly gone where no man had gone before.

Sami worked her clit firmly with his tongue, humming slightly as she licked and sucked his cock. The vibrations from his humming must have gone all the way through her pelvis to Hari's finger, because he started to move it very carefully within her.

The sexual arousal she was experiencing was immense—if she didn't come soon it was going to be all over.

Her two lovers seemed to sense her agony.

Sami's tongue flickered at the speed of a hummingbird's wings over her clit, and Hari pressed, pushed and pleasured her anus with his fingers while she slithered her cleft over his cock and sucked for all she was worth on Sami.

The three of them hung, poised for a lifetime on the edge, then with a scream, Alana came and the world pretty much ended.

* * * * *

Or, on the other hand, she may just have blacked out for a few moments, she thought, as she struggled back to a state of limp but satisfied consciousness. Three sets of limbs were boneless and tangled, and large amounts of blue fog were hanging over everything.

Alana couldn't help herself — she grinned. As soon as she had the use of her body back, she was going to high-five both of them — she had never, in her entire life, felt as good as she did at this moment. It didn't matter that she had all the muscular strength of an amoeba with the flu, or that she was lying in the wettest wet spot she could remember. What was important was that she'd achieved a level of sexual arousal she'd never believed possible, *and* helped the guys get off at the same time.

Yep. That was definitely a grin-worthy moment.

Hari stirred behind her, and Sami's head moved away from her clit.

Both men groaned slightly as they sorted out their arms and legs and pulled pillows into more comfortable positions for all of them.

"So," croaked Alana, as she looked from Sami on one side of her to Hari on the other. "Did I pass?"

Chapter Eight

She awoke to find herself draped over a hard male chest. A deep breath told her it was Hari—funny how she could distinguish them by their scent. Sami's was a mixture of sweet and tangy—sort of like a spice—while Hari's was a more robust fragrance, redolent of male and heat. She remembered her question of last night. Had she passed? Hari had mumbled something that sounded like "class valedictorian" as he had cleaned the sticky juices off them all with soft, scented cloths. But Sami had surprised her the most.

He had slid his hands through her hair and brought her head to his—lowering his lips to hers in the first fully-fledged kiss she could remember getting from either of them. His lips were warm and sweet and he gently increased their pressure as he moved his fingers lovingly through her tousled curls. As she had opened her lips, his tongue had slipped inside and proved that he was as talented at kissing as he was at everything else.

He tasted of Blue Lotus, Sami, and desire, and he swirled his tongue lovingly against hers with consummate skill.

She should have known. His kiss warmed her, touched her deep inside, and she felt cherished as he eased himself away.

"Thank you, Alana," he'd said, his emotions laid bare in his amazing blue eyes. "You're very special."

Not quite sure how to respond, Alana simply leaned forward and kissed him back.

He'd smiled, turned her toward Hari and spooned himself in behind her. All three had fallen asleep within moments.

Now Sami was off someplace doing heaven knew what, and she was sprawled in the bed with one arm over Hari's chest, her leg resting on his thighs, and her lips almost touching one muscled shoulder. Mmmmm. This was a nice way to wake up.

"Good morning, Alana," came a deep voice, rumbling through her body as well as her ears.

"Hi, Hari," she smiled, riffling his chest hair with her fingers.

"Are you ready to begin the second phase of your instruction today?"

"Bring it on, Professor," laughed Alana. "What's on the curriculum?"

Hari eased his body away from her and grasped the sheet, drawing it down and away from her body. He took his time, staring pointedly at each part of her that was revealed.

"Hari?" she asked, surprisingly conscious of her nakedness. "What is the second part of the course? What does it involve?"

"Fucking."

The one word answer brought a flood of adrenaline through her veins, and she was suddenly wide awake.

"Um — and we haven't been doing that already?"

"Oh no, my delight," murmured Hari, rolling her onto her back.

He placed his hand just under her navel and spread his long fingers across her abdomen. The warmth penetrated through her pelvis to her womb.

"We've had fun, and played, and come but we haven't really *fucked*. That's my portion of the session. I get to teach you about your inner self. Those lush and tight and silky places that make your juices. I'm going to get those places so hot and wet you'll think there's a volcano inside you." His fingers flexed slightly as he moved upwards and gazed into Alana's eyes.

"My cock is going to slam into your pussy until you scream from the pleasure of it. I'm going to take you many times and in many ways. I'm going to fuck you until all you can think about is how hard my cock is and how you can get it inside you."

Alana's eyes widened as she stared at Hari. His chocolate gaze was burning, his dark hair tumbled over his shoulders and he looked like sex incarnate. He was turning her on with just his words. This was a major switch from the lighthearted loving fun she'd experienced with Sami's fingers and tongue. This was sex on the Dark Side.

"Lead on, Lord Vader," she murmured, conscious now of her pussy beginning to weep at his words.

"I'm going to take you every way I can and everywhere I can. I'm gonna live inside your cunt for a while…"

Alana gasped as Hari's lips curled.

"Yeah—that word. I don't really like it, and we've stayed away from it up to now, but this is the advanced course—no kindergarten terms any more. You've made the extra credit class, sweetheart, and this is where the fucking gets real."

She swallowed. "And Sami?"

Hari moved between her thighs, resting his cock on her curls. The sensation was exquisite.

"Sure. He'll be here—he'll watch us and help out occasionally, he might even want to fuck you himself now and again. But make no mistake, Alana, it's going to be my cock that slams you into oblivion."

He gestured at his cock, which was enormous—the flared head was tinged with purple and glittering drops of bluish moisture were sliding down from the slit.

"You're going to stretch for me, hold me tight between your thighs. You're going to learn my rhythm as I learn yours. My cock is going to force its way into your most secret places and pound them into screaming submission. You'll yearn for it when it's not inside you— you'll suck it and lick it, you may even make me come that way if you're very good. But the best part will be having me inside you, sliding into and out of your wet cunt, slapping against your pussy, pounding into your clit. My cock is going to rule your body for a while Alana—get used to it."

And suiting words to action, he slammed into her body all the way to the hilt.

Alana's breath left her lungs in a rush. He was huge, and she felt stretched taut.

Hari's eyes gazed into hers as he froze, motionless, above her. He was deep inside her, yet his words had aroused her to the extent where she had been quite ready to take him.

Uncertainly, she watched his face.

Gradually he eased back from her and closed his eyes, thrusting in again and out, setting up the most delicious vibrations throughout her whole body.

Alana's buttocks clenched and she raised herself slightly to give him better access. His movements quickened, and she could feel the tension rising within her as his body pounded against her clit and his balls slapped her buttocks with every thrust.

In moments, she felt the orgasm start and she raised her hands to grip Hari's muscular biceps.

"Oh God," she whimpered, head and neck arching back into the pillow.

Hari's pounding speeded up—just enough.

"Aaaagh…" she groaned as her orgasm began and her cunt spasmed against Hari's thick cock.

He pressed himself in as deep as he could go, letting her muscles massage him and waiting out her climax.

As she came down, Hari eased gently out of her.

"That was lesson number one, Alana. Nicely done."

"And for having an excellent orgasm first thing in the morning, the lucky lady wins…Ta Da. One cup of tantalizingly fresh steaming coffee." Sami's cheerful tones cut through the post-coital fog that was swirling between Alana's ears.

"But wait, there's more," continued Sami, doing an excellent impression of every game show host she'd ever heard. Her lips started to curve, as did Hari's.

"You and a guest will spend minutes of untold pleasure enjoying a breakfast prepared especially for you. Grapes imported for your delectation from the Hanging Gardens of Babylon, figs specially flown in from the fourth century, and oranges fresh from the trees of an Arabic Sheik."

"Fruit for breakfast again, huh?" snorted Hari, lunging off the bed at Sami. "What about pancakes? What about eggs and bacon? Haven't you heard of Aunt Jemima?"

"Fruit, my brother, and you know it. Better for you, and better for what you're going to be doing..." Sami nodded firmly at Alana who was trying to figure out a way to get all her body parts working at once.

"Yeah, yeah..." complained Hari. "Where's the coffee?"

* * * * *

As it turned out, the coffee was, indeed, fresh, hot and delicious. Alana was getting used to the stronger and darker brew, almost Turkish in its richness. She smacked her lips and groaned in appreciation as the first sip went down.

"Oh God, that's divine. Fantastic sex and great coffee. Can I marry you both? Take me somewhere where I can have two husbands, and you're mine, guys."

Hari and Sami exchanged grins across the table.

"You are happy that we have come to you?" asked Sami.

"God! See this? This is my 'you've-got-to-be-kidding' face. You have taken me places I never dreamed existed. How could I not be happy?" she answered.

"And you don't mind that it is I who will be the one fucking you?" Hari's voice was surprisingly hesitant as he asked this question. Alana realized the answer was important to him, and to Sami.

"Listen up, you two. You are both essential parts of this fantasy or dream, or hallucination, or whatever it is I'm enjoying the hell out of. Whatever Sami does to me is marvelous, and whatever you do to me, Hari, is going to be just as good, and what you both do to me—well, there aren't words for it. Trust me."

A thought crossed her mind.

"Do you always work like this? Sami first, then Hari?"

Sami answered that one. "We note our roles when we conclude each assignment, Alana. We have a chart in our quarters that we fill out and when next we are assigned, we know to reverse the procedure. On our next case, I will be the one to fuck the client, while Hari will get to use his other talents."

"That's us," muttered Hari. "The suck and fuck twins."

"Hari?" said Alana, sensing that Hari was not altogether thrilled with the arrangement.

"Forgive me, Alana, it is not you. It is just that sometimes, in our quarters, we wonder if there is not something more—or if we are destined to spend eternity going from one client to another, never remembering the warmth or the love that we share with her…"

Alana reached out and grasped both their hands. "I wish I could find a way to help with that problem," she said, "because I want you to remember how much I've come to love you both."

As she said the words she knew they were true. These two gorgeous, metaphysically impossible men had worked their magical way into her heart with their loving and touching and above all, their caring.

A thought flashed through her mind.

"What am I going to do without you?" Her eyes filled with tears. "Oh God, how am I going to let you go?"

Sami cleared his throat awkwardly and Hari looked down at the table, both clearly affected by Alana's cry.

"If I just stop coming, will that mean you'll have to stay longer?" she asked, looking at Hari and then at Sami.

"It doesn't work that way, my delight," answered Sami sadly. "As we sleep, our experiences are...are...I guess the best way to describe it is 'downloaded' by our Guardian—he monitors our progress with you. That's how we knew it was time to move on to the next phase."

"You mean somebody is watching us?"

"Not exactly," said Hari. "He is the Guardian, and it is his assigned duty to keep an eye on his Djinns—for our safety as much as anything else."

"Hmmm...sounds like a case of 'Big Djinn' is watching, to me." Alana got up from the table and moved to wash her mug in the sink. Her mind was in turmoil, buzzing and worrying and turning this problem over and over. She hadn't gotten to be a successful small businesswoman without coming up with some innovative ideas. Somehow she had to do something for Hari and Sami. What that something was, she didn't quite know yet, but she was determined—she had a goal. God help anything or anybody that stood in her way.

Without thinking, she hit the remote for her stereo—a routine move she'd been doing every morning at her sink for years. Strains of the Bee Gees filled the air.

Before the Brothers Gibb could announce that you could tell they were men from the way they walked, Hari and Sami had the table pushed back and were moving— discoing actually, in her kitchen. Alana's mouth dropped.

They were good. No, strike that, they were great. Chippendales could have cleared a fortune off these guys.

Two sets of strong arms swung to the disco beat and two sets of feet whirled and stomped. Sami twisted and turned—Michael Jackson and Paula Abdul would have eaten their hearts out for some of his moves.

Like Travolta, he dropped to his knees and bounded back up again, strutting in rhythm like a dude with a bad case of *Saturday Night Fever*. But if Sami was the showman, Hari was the *Lord of the Dance*.

Elegant and austere, his moves were more sensual— his muscles danced as much as his body did—and when they both turned around and waggled their butts at her, it was too much.

Her mouth watered, and she wanted nothing more than to take a bite out of those wonderful firm cheeks, even though they happened to be clad in pants at that moment.

The Village People were now lauding the benefits of the *Y.M.C.A.* What the heck had gotten into her radio station, anyway? Disco nostalgia?

Alana burst out laughing as both Hari and Sami broke into an amazingly lifelike routine to the belting rhythm of the song. Her feet tapped on the floor and she clapped her hands, giggling as Sami bobbled his eyebrows in time to the beat.

The sound of Alana's doorbell froze everyone in their tracks—with the exception of the Village People, of course, who had never frozen for a second since 1969.

Sami hurriedly turned the volume down.

"Oh shit—did you shield this place?"

"No—I thought you did."

"I thought you did. Omar's balls!"

"Damn."

"Sorry, Alana," said Hari, turning to her. "We usually don't make so much noise— or at least if we do, we put up a shield so that we don't disturb anybody else. I guess this time we forgot…"

The doorbell rang again.

"Oh well—no harm done. I'll just go soothe whichever of my neighbors is going to complain," she grinned.

"Just a moment, Alana," said Sami, waving his hands.

Her old sweats disappeared, to be replaced by her silk caftan and *cushi* bell. She raised an eyebrow.

Both guys grinned at her encouragingly. "If you're going to be our most successful Sex Goddess yet, you might as well start dressing like one."

"Yeah, right," she snorted.

"Remember, Alana—whoever it is cannot see us," whispered Hari as she went to the door.

Peeking through her security lens, she saw an unwelcome sight. Sighing, she opened the door.

"Hello, George."

Chapter Nine

She stood quietly in the doorway surveying her unwelcome guest.

George had become convinced, somewhere along the line, that women adored him. Whoever had given him that impression should either be locked up or shot, thought Alana to herself. She noted the wet-looking, slicked back hair, which still managed to stick out over his ears, the muscle shirt (which could have used a good bleaching), and the jeans—tight, but not fitting the way they should. Not the way Sami's fit, for example. She sighed, knowing that such a comparison was *really* unfair.

"Hiya, sweets—heard the music and figured you must be setting up a going away party for me."

He slithered past Alana and into her apartment before she had a chance to protest and made his way into the kitchen. Alana noted the table was back in its usual place and there was no sign of her two visitors—she had no idea if they could turn invisible and were still in the room or what. Shrugging mentally, she turned her attention to George.

"You're leaving?" she said, trying to keep the joyful note out of her voice.

"Yeppers. Moving out this afternoon. Gotta keep up with the market, babes."

He leaned against the counter in what he probably believed was a sexy pose. Actually, all it did was thrust a portion of white flesh out through the gap in the top of his jeans—yeah, they were unfastened, sheesh, was it a guy thing? His muscle shirt would have been okay if there had been any muscles within a mile or so of its vicinity. Unfortunately, the muscle fairy had not blessed George, and the shirt kept trying to slide off his narrow shoulders. Probably *trying desperately to escape*, thought Alana whimsically. *What was I thinking when I let this man touch me?*

"You were lonely, Alana. That's not a crime," whispered a soft voice in her ear. Jerking slightly, she moved to a chair and sat down, trying to remember George's last comment.

"And that market would be…"

George laughed, trying for a deep chuckle and achieving a mid-range squawk. "Hey, plumbing supplies, honey. Remember I told you about the building boom going on upstate? We opened a branch office up there and I'm being transferred as manager. Aren't you going to congratulate me?"

He wiggled his eyebrows in what he must have imagined was a real sexy turn-on kind of way. It actually resembled two woolly caterpillars doing the tango on his broad forehead, especially with that one extra long brow hair that stuck out…no, best not go there. Alana mentally pushed her breakfast back down, and gave a polite smile.

"I'm very pleased for your good fortune, George. I'm sure this is a great step up for you. Congratulations."

"Now honeycakes, that's not what I had in mind…" he leered. "See, here's me about to leave for bigger and better things, and here's you looking —I gotta say it— looking mighty fine this morning. Oh yes, *mighty* fine…"

His eyes roved hotly over Alana's body. She knew that the soft silk was clinging to her nipples and guessed it was pretty obvious to George that she had little or nothing on underneath.

The front of his jeans swelled. A little.

His fingers went to his zip. "See, I was thinking more along the lines of you and me getting horizontal, ya know?"

The sound of the zip going down was paralleled by one of Alana's eyebrows going up.

"Really? As I recall, there wasn't very much 'horizontal' about anything, last time I allowed you in here," she responded acidly.

"Hey — gotta try new stuff, babes. It was kinda fun."

"Gosh — really? I suppose it must have been. They say time flies when you're having fun. It seemed like, what, all of about fifteen seconds?"

"Aw, don't blame me if you didn't see stars, sweetcakes. Sometimes girls just don't make it. Why don't you let me an' Junior here have a go at making it better."

George gestured to his cock, which was now half-heartedly waving at her. George had apparently forgotten or already packed his underwear. The thought of Hari or Sami without underwear made her mouth water. The thought of George without underwear made her want Alka Seltzer. Fast.

"This is your love tool, babe. Come and say hi to Junior — you know what he is?"

Taking the wind out of George's sails, Alana answered before he could go into his spiel about his cock being the answer to the troubles of every woman within a radius of ten miles.

"Yes, I think I know what that is, George. It looks like a penis. Only smaller."

Junior didn't like that, and shrank slightly in embarrassment.

"Hey—no need to get mean, sweets, just because you can't hit the big O every time, like some of us here…" Junior got an encouraging stroke and perked up a little. "Like I said, it takes practice. So whaddya say you come over here and let me slide my hands under that cute little dress of yours, huh? Come give George a real send-off."

Alana sent up a prayer to heaven that, just for a few minutes, murder would be quite legal.

Drawing a deep breath she swayed across the room, making her *cushi* bell tinkle and feeling her self-confidence build with each step.

George's face betrayed his rising excitement. "Hey— you're ringing my chimes, sweet lips," he said, staring at her breasts as they moved gently beneath her gown.

"Oh yeah, oh yeah…" he said as she reached for his pants and freed him from the fabric.

"Oh that's more like it, toots—go for it. Give Junior a big old kiss, why doncha?"

Alana gritted her teeth. God, she was going to shower for a week after this. She reached lower and found George's balls, compactly tucked against his body. She eased them free and into the cool air of the kitchen.

George sighed and widened his stance, eyes closed and waiting for her to go down on him.

His eyes flew open as Alana slowly tightened her grasp.

"Hey—whoa—easy, babe—you've got the future generations of my family there..."

"Oh God, don't let him tempt me like this," she murmured.

"Be cautious, Alana-love, you can inflict great damage without caution," warned Sami's soft voice in her ear.

"I'd be doing womankind a favor," she responded.

"Wha—What favor?" stuttered George, trying to keep pace with Alana's words, while his balls were held in an ever-tightening grip. His hands clenched the counter on either side of him and he froze as her fingers increased their pressure.

"George, you and I have to have a little dialogue," she said politely.

"Oh—er—you mean like talk about stuff before we do it?" said George, hopefully.

"Not exactly." Her fingers tightened ever so slightly.

George blinked.

"See, George, I think you skipped a couple of classes in sex ed. I think you and Junior here were so busy trying to get someone to do it with you that you missed learning how it should be done."

"Hah. I've never had any complaints, babe. I think you're off base there," he answered, as confidently as he could for a man with his balls in the equivalent of a wringer.

"Well, for instance, George, a woman has feelings. She has mental feelings and physical feelings." Alana moved slightly getting herself more comfortable and giving another little twist to the package in her hand.

Junior scurried into hiding.

"Her mental feelings require you to make sure she wants to 'do it' *before* you actually go ahead and start doing it. That might involve something as simple as asking her if she wants sex, or perhaps even complimenting her body and saying nice things. Are you with me so far, George?"

Twist.

"Yessss," hissed George.

"Good. Now there are also physical feelings, George. That means that her body would like to be touched in certain places. They're called, and I'm going to use a very big word here, George, so pay attention, they're called 'Erogenous Zones.' Do you think you could remember that?" *Twist.*

"Uh huh!" squeaked George.

"So in the future, you'll remember to perhaps touch or even kiss a woman's breasts, George."

Junior displayed some interest at the direction of the conversation. Alana had to give him points for single-mindedness.

"And there are other places she might like to be touched as well. It's kind of up to you to find out, but a good suggestion is to gently stroke around and see what she likes. And you can tell when she's ready for you, George. Do you know how?" *Squeeze.*

George nodded, swallowing noisily.

"Good, but I'm going to tell you anyway, in case you've got it wrong. After you've spent some time touching her, George—and I mean time, not two minutes per breast and three everywhere else, but real quality time—she's going to start to warm up. That's start, George, just start. Not 'Okay I'm ready, stick it in me,

George,' a woman's body doesn't work like that. Are you still with me?" *Twist.*

Sweat beaded George's upper lip.

"You'll find she gets wet, George, very wet. And that's when you know she's ready for you...*not before.*"

George nodded again, biting his lip.

"I hear you, Alana," he groaned.

Alana glanced down to see that Junior was busily trying to hide himself, in fact if he hid any more he'd be backing out of George's ass.

She released her grip a tiny bit and George sucked in a breath of air.

"Now, I don't know where you're moving to, George, and I don't want to know. But I'd like to think that I have improved things for the girls you're gonna be dating in the future, and if you remember what I've told you here today, some of them might even enjoy having sex with you and want to do it again. That would probably be a first, wouldn't it, George?"

"Well...I..."

The fingers tightened again.

"Yes, yes...okay, you're right. Women don't go out with me twice, okay?"

"See? I'm doing you a huge favor here, George. Now, I think this lecture is about over, and it's time for you and Junior to take your leave. But there is one thing I'd like you to know..."

She leaned in really close and breathed in George's ear.

"If you ever try and stick it to a woman before she's ready and willing like you did to me that night, I'm going to find you, George. And I'm going to bring along some of my own plumbing supplies. I think a nice length of 2-1/2 inch PVC tubing ought to do the job. And do you know what I'm going to do with that, George?"

Wisely, he made no comment, just shook his head.

"I'm going to ram it so far up your ass that it'll drain your sinuses and you'll never have to blow your nose again. You clear on that, George? I mean crystal clear?"

Alana punctuated her question with a definite jerk on his balls and George turned white. Only the fear that he might throw up on her deterred her from inflicting the pain she felt he so richly deserved.

"It's time to go, George, just follow me."

She left him little choice, as she still held his balls in a grip of iron. George shuffled behind her in abject terror.

Opening the front door, Alana "encouraged" him to leave by dragging her hand through the door, correctly assuming that where his balls were, George would be right behind.

Finally, she released her hand, just managing to stop herself from wiping it on her lovely silk caftan. Ugh. Nut cooties.

"Now look here..." blustered George, feeling righteous macho indignation returning along with the feeling to his scrotum.

"Sleep, you ignorant pile of camel dung." A whisper came from behind Alana.

George's eyes rolled back in his head and he slithered to the ground.

"Oh, nice touch, guys. Can you teach me to do that?"

Hari and Sami emerged, grinning, and tugged him a short way down the hall, leaving him resting in a semi upright position with his fly wide open. Junior was tucked away in terror and the sight of George with his package hanging out was not one to increase his reputation as a stud.

Alana giggled, and then looked at her hand.

"Aargh."

Hari and Sami closed the door behind them and found Alana in the kitchen, fiercely scrubbing her hands with disinfectant soap.

"I can't believe I touched him—he's bound to have nut cooties—oh, God, I'll never get this hand clean."

Sami quirked a brow. "Nut cooties?"

"Yeah—nasty little thingies that stay on your hands after you've touched someone's really gross nuts…"

"Never heard of them," said Hari. "Do we have them?"

Alana gasped out a laugh.

"Dear God, no. Cooties would kill for the privilege of being on your nuts, guys," she laughed, and then clapped a hand over her mouth when she realized what she'd said.

"Geez, what's gotten into me? I'm grabbing people by the balls, and talking about cootie nuts…I'm still hallucinating all this, aren't I?"

The two Djinns sat at her table and watched as she finished the decontamination of her hand.

"Alana, you are not hallucinating. You are simply becoming more confident in yourself as a woman. You are beginning to realize that there is a very sexual person inside you and she's got to be free to be a part of you."

Alana thought about that for a minute.

"I wonder if you're right. It did feel fantastic to be able to get that George business out of my system. He really hurt me, and it felt good to tell him why. I really had his attention, didn't I?" she grinned.

Both Hari and Sami shifted on their chairs.

"I would say that was a fairly accurate assessment of the situation, Alana, yes," answered Hari. "We felt for the poor man, actually. You do know that you were hanging on to one of the most delicate areas of a man's body, don't you?"

Alana snorted.

"Of course. Why do you think I did it? How else could I get him to listen—short of physical violence? I needed to make a point, and I had to use the weapon at hand, which was—" she flexed her fingers, "—my hand."

"And a beautiful hand it is, too…" said Sami, crossing to her and picking it up. "May I finish your cleansing routine for you?"

He raised her hand to his lips and began to suck and lick each of her fingers, running his warm tongue over each groove and curve.

She shivered as he placed a final kiss on her pinky.

"We never finished our dance, Alana," murmured Hari, waving his hands and nodding at Sami.

"The space is now shielded—let's—what's the word— 'groove'."

Turning up the radio, the sounds of the Rolling Stones thumped into the room. Before she knew it, Alana was naked except for her *cushi* bell, along with both Sami and

Hari, who were swaying to the earthy beat of *Honky Tonk Woman*.

Sami pulled her with him into the living room.

"Dirty dancing is about to begin, Alana-love, are you ready?"

He pulled her hips tight against him as Hari thrust at her from behind. She was the filling in a Djinn Oreo. She had never been happier.

Chapter Ten

They danced. Oh—did they dance. Alana couldn't remember the last time she'd danced like this, but thought that perhaps it might have been her junior high prom.

Twisting and sliding to Mick and the boys belting out "Satisfaction," Alana laughed aloud as she shook her hips. There was a tremendously liberating feeling about dancing nude—it was sort of like skinny-dipping (which she'd done exactly once in her entire life, at a friend's pool under cover of darkness).

This celebration of rhythm, however, was something else again.

Of course, the fact that two lip-licking gorgeous male bodies were brushing up against hers all the time might have had something to do with it—and the fact that they were both getting really nice hard-ons from the touches was a kick, too.

The music changed—the beat slowed and the drum picked up. Suddenly it wasn't Mick any more, but probably Ahmed and the Camel Ravers.

"Now we will show you how *we* dirty dance, Alana-delight," panted Sami.

"The beat is carried by the *dumbeg*, or drum," said Hari, closing the space between their bodies. From behind her he reached around and held her hipbones in his strong hands.

"It's covered with camel skin, and the drummer holds it firmly between his knees, the way a woman holds a man when he's deep inside her and throbbing like a drum…"

Hari's hands pressed and moved against her hips. She found herself moving along with him, swaying in a loose movement in time with the beat.

She heard the different tones of the drum as Hari helped her hips thrust more— first to one side then the other. She felt like the most exhibitionistic belly dancer as her *cushi* bell jingled wildly in response to her hips.

"Listen to the drum talk, Alana…" he encouraged.

"Dum tek-a-tek, tek-a-dum dum tek-a-tek…" Hari breathed the words along with the beat the drummer was pounding out.

A musical riff threaded through the air over the beat of the drum.

"And now the *oud*," said Sami, brushing his hands from her shoulders to her wrists.

"An *oud*? It sounds like a mandolin or a—what's that Russian instrument—oh yes, a balalaika."

Sami pulled her arms away from her body and raised them into the classic dance pose above her head. He interlaced her fingers and helped her arms flow in time to the music, freely and seductively.

"An *oud* is many thousands of years old. It is believed to have come from Mesopotamia, but no matter where it started, it's part of our music—in fact most music of the Middle East. It's the father of the lute and other instruments, but nothing quite sounds as fundamental as the *dumbeg* and the *oud*, especially when a woman is dancing to them."

Hari's hands slid off her hips and down toward her groin, still pulling and pushing her into figure eights and incidentally making her pussy tighten and relax in a very stimulating way.

Sami's chest brushed against her nipples. They stiffened and she felt the air caressing them as they moved with her body to the beat of the drum.

Then both Sami and Hari let go.

"Let your body take over, Alana — dance the *shifte telli* with us..." said Hari, slithering his back seductively up and down hers as he bent low at the knees. He held his arms wide and snapped his fingers on the beat.

Sami did the same, turning his back and glancing over his shoulder at her as he caressed her breasts with his hard flesh. She felt the moisture pooling between her thighs, and her hips rolled all by themselves.

"This is a dance of seduction, Alana-love," murmured Hari. "You are the slave maiden who must convince your master that you are worthy of being his concubine."

Alana closed her eyes and swayed, the thump of the drum echoing the thump of her blood through her veins.

"You must seduce him with your dancing, your skin, your breasts, your hips, show him that if he should deign to fuck you he will never want for another woman — you can be his harem of one."

Caught up in the fantasy, Alana let herself go.

The drum pounded, the *oud* cried out its passionate song and Alana danced.

Danced like she never had before.

Her arms caressed Hari and Sami then swept across her own breasts. She turned and rubbed her back and buttocks against male flesh, feeling their cocks firm and aroused against her. Her hips couldn't keep still, as if the drums were inside her pelvis and she had to thrust and gyrate to keep the rhythm going.

She felt her heart pounding and the sweat breaking out on her brow, but she kept on, watching Hari and Sami as they too began to feel the sensuality of the dance.

Their cocks hardened even more, they licked their lips and panted, beads of moisture rolling down across their broad shoulders.

Swaying hips and swaying cocks—Alana was mesmerized. Finally, the need for full contact overcame her and she turned her back on Hari, thrusting and swinging her buttocks backwards toward his crotch and leaning against his chest.

His hands automatically grasped her and slid toward her curls.

Sami raised his arms and touched her hands, putting them around the back of his neck. His fingers released hers and followed the undersides of her arms to the sides of her breasts.

The drumbeat roared to a crescendo. Alana's hips shimmied and shook, feeling Hari's cock sliding over her butt and around and through and between and everywhere except where she desperately needed it to be.

With a rolling conclusion the drums finished, and Hari fell back toward the couch, dragging Alana with him.

It took one thrust and he was inside her—oh so deep inside her. The heat of his body pressed against her back as she sat on his lap, his thighs between hers spreading them wide. She felt the air on her swollen tissues and moaned as Hari's hands came around to spread her flesh apart and feather touches on her aroused clit.

Sami stood before her, but didn't kneel to her pussy as she'd expected.

Instead he placed his hands on either side of her breasts and pushed them together. They were just the right height.

With a move any belly dancer would have envied, Sami thrust his cock up between her breasts with a gasp of pleasure. He palmed her nipples as Hari bounced her on his cock and ran his fingers over her now frantic clit.

Sami and Hari moved to their own syncopated rhythm—Hari's upthrust in concert with Sami's downpull.

Alana felt she had no say in the matter, but honestly didn't care. She was trembling on the edge of a mighty orgasm—who cared who was doing what to whom, she just needed to come, dammit.

Hari deepened his penetration, along with his fingers, driving her entire nervous system into a state of panic.

Sami's thrusts brought the tip of his cock just to her chin, which clearly did wonderful things for Sami—she felt a drop of his juices moistening her skin as the swollen head brushed against her. His balls swung heavily against her torso.

Alana's buttocks clenched in arousal, her juices flooding Hari's thighs. He spread his legs even further, stretching Alana's pussy to the limit and sending her clit into spasms of ecstasy as the little pearl jutted out and away from her body—swollen and sensitive and oh-so-ready to meet the sure touch of Hari's slippery fingers.

Sami moaned and closed his eyes.

They broke within moments, and there was fog. A lot of fog.

* * * * *

Alana coughed and Hari's relaxing cock slid wetly out of her.

"Geez, guys, this fog thing…" She waved her hands to clear the air, trying to pull a breath into her panting lungs.

Hari unpeeled himself from her back, and Sami turned slightly from where he'd collapsed facedown on the couch next to her.

"I'm hungry," said Sami, still not moving his body. "I'm completely wiped out, but by the Gods I could eat a camel."

"Sorry, I'm all out of camel. How about frozen pizza?"

Hari's eyes lit up, but Sami frowned.

"Not today, Alana-love. Today we must treat the body as a temple and offer nutrition that will enhance and improve its overall performance. Pizza—" and he slanted a grimace at Hari, "pizza will only fill your stomach and slow your digestive system. You will be depleted of the energies you will need for tonight."

Alana, who had been listening to Sami with one ear while the other registered the fact that her heart was actually approaching a normal rhythm again, dropped her head forward and closed her eyes.

"Dear heavens above—I haven't the energy…" she moaned.

Hari grinned. "You will have, dear one, never fear. But Sami is right—we need a slightly different routine to prepare for this evening."

He shifted to his feet and pulled Alana up with him.

"A nice shower will restore your balance—and while you are doing that, Sami and I will prepare a list of things for you to buy for us. It is acceptable for you?"

Alana looked at the two of them, and humphed.

"Providing you keep it simple—no camel balls or anything."

Sami looked quite green.

"Not me. I hate those."

"You don't mean you actually eat...Oh God, never mind. I'm gone."

Hari's rich laugh followed her into the shower, where she found the guys had been right—she felt full of life and ready to take on the world.

Of course, there was one thing missing—her clothes. Her closets had mysteriously emptied themselves, along with her dresser. She knew she should be irate, but had a hard time summoning up anger for these two wonders who clearly had her best interests at heart.

Sighing, she wrapped herself in her towel and went to do battle with her two clothing-impaired guests.

She found them in the kitchen, fresh coffee in their mugs and a list on the table next to her cup.

"Um, fellas—about this clothing thing—I can't shop in just a *cushi* bell, and I think a silk caftan and nothing else would attract the wrong kind of attention at the market."

"No problem..." said Hari, studying her for a moment and then waving his hand.

Gasping, Alana felt clothes materialize on her body. A really strange sensation. Looking down, she saw she was now the proud possessor of a nice pair of denim cutoffs, cut a little shorter around the butt than she was used to, but otherwise a perfect fit. They were topped with a cropped top in a delicate blue floral print, and left a nice expanse of midriff bare. Her chain twinkled on the bare skin.

"Well—so far so good, but haven't you forgotten something?"

"Ooops, sorry..." said Hari, snapping his fingers.

A lovely pair of openwork leather sandals appeared on her feet. Soft and comfortable, Alana realized she'd never had shoes that felt so wonderful. Hey—could they do Ferragamos?

"Do you guys do designer knockoffs?"

"Pardon?"

Alana sighed. It would be a challenge, and she wasn't sure if she was up to it.

"Actually, I was talking about underwear. You haven't created any."

Two identically evil grins crossed their faces.

"That's right."

"Why bother? You don't need it."

"Hey—excuse me, this isn't the South Pacific. It gets damn cold here in the winter, and I'm not running around with my butt cheeks hanging out when it's ten below zero," complained Alana, hands on hips.

Sami chuckled, and Hari leaned back in his chair with a smile on his face.

"We're not suggesting any such thing, Alana. We are simply helping you explore your sexual side—a side that, now and again, skips the whole constricting underwear thing. Your breasts are beautiful—firm and upright, with nipples that would make Sheba envious. Why restrain them in your equivalent of armor when you are not going into battle, only to the store?"

"And as far as panties go—which isn't far…" added Hari, "today is a lovely warm day, the sun is shining and you'll only be gone for a short time. Why ruin the line of those lovely shorts by slipping anything between them and that soft skin that covers your woman's treasures?"

Her "woman's treasures" throbbed and dampened.

Alana sighed. "Gimme the list. I'd better get out of here, before you talk me into naked grocery shopping as an acceptable hobby."

She looked at the scrawled words and frowned.

"Sorry—my ancient Arabic is kind of rusty—any chance you could write this in English?"

"Oh—Omar's balls. Sorry, Alana." Hari quickly wrote a new list that she could read.

"Hmm. Mostly fruits, I see. I think I can get these for you—I don't know about the fresh figs, though…I'll have to check. If it was Saturday, I could get most of this from the market, but seeing as it's…what the heck day is it, anyway?"

Sami looked self-conscious and glanced at Hari.

"Actually it is still Saturday, Alana."

Silence fell in the room as Alana's brain refused to accept that statement.

"But…but—I've slept—we've slept. It's been days that you've been here. I've seen the sun rise and set…I don't understand…" she almost wailed in her confusion.

Hari left his chair and came around the table, drawing Alana to her feet. He enfolded her in his strong arms and cuddled her into his chest. She felt Sami behind her, running his fingers gently through her hair.

"Don't be disturbed, Alana-love," gentled Hari in his most seductive tones.

"We don't truly understand it ourselves. But there is something about our presence that affects the passage of time. While we are with you, time passes at a different rate. It allows us to spend as long as is necessary with you without seriously impacting the rest of your life or that of your world."

Sami's hand continued its soft stroking.

"Time has not stopped, Alana, merely slowed to a different rate while we are here," added Sami. "There is no reason to be distraught—we do not like it when you are upset like this…"

Alana sighed.

"I suppose I should have expected something like this. Everything else is kind of weird and strange, why not time itself. Maybe I'll see if I can find *Temporal Distortion for Dummies* while I'm out."

Hari cocked his head.

"What are these books for dummies you mention? Are there so many dummies in your world?"

Alana chuckled against his wonderful chest.

"Probably yes, but never mind. Some things in my world aren't easily explained either." She pulled herself away.

"I'm okay now—it was just a shock, that's all. Give me the list and I'll head to the fruit market. What are you two going to do?"

"Well, laundry might be an option," groaned Sami.

"You mean you can't just wave your hands and—poof—clean shorts?"

"We don't wear shorts, Alana, have you forgotten already?" Hari's voice dropped to the dark chocolate level. "Perhaps I should remind you?"

His hand dropped suggestively to the bulge in his jeans and the ever-open top button.

"No, for heavens sake, keep that tucked away for a while, will ya? I need to shop and take a break here…" She sighed.

"Don't be long, Alana-delight," murmured Sami. "We will miss your arousing presence while you're gone."

Alana licked her lips and wondered if she could talk them into frozen pizza after all. Her nipples were already hard as could be and thrusting against the soft cotton of her top—she was a walking ad for Sex and Plenty Of It. Plus, her *cushi* bell was held tight against her pussy by the shorts and was giving her a little thrill with every step she took. God, this was going to be one hell of a shopping trip.

Chapter Eleven

Alana struggled through the door clutching three brown paper bags full of fruits and one obligatory loaf of French bread — her indulgence for the weekend. Food wise, anyway.

Her apartment was silent.

"Hey guys," she called, dumping her burdens on the kitchen table. "I got your stuff. No fresh figs, but I got a packet of dried instead. Is that okay? Guys?"

A cold hand clawed at her heart as silence reigned.

"Oh God, no! Please...don't leave me yet! Please — no!"

With her heart in her mouth, she rushed into the living room to find it empty. Really scared now, she hurried into her bedroom only to stop short on a gasp.

Gone was her traditional room with its sleigh bed and fuzzy rug. In its place was a mystical and brilliant white space.

The walls were covered from floor to ceiling with a floating kind of drapery, sheer and billowing as she moved past. The floors were white marble, with delicate gold-veined tracery through them — she impulsively kicked her sandals off, needing to feel the cool smoothness beneath her feet.

A large futon had replaced her bed and had been moved into the center of the room. Much thicker than ones she had seen in the past, it was covered with a gleaming white satin comforter that just begged to be snuggled in. Very large cushions were casually tossed here and there—the kind that decorator magazines used to great effect—and these were also white, finished with large and ornate golden tassels.

Brass containers had been placed against the walls—heavy white candles in some of them. A huge, thick, white animal skin rug lay casually next to the futon—what kind of animal it was, Alana couldn't begin to guess—the abominable snowman?

She brushed her toe through the silken strands as her eyes half closed against the brilliant glare.

"Look up, Alana," said a voice, and in an instant Hari and Sami were on either side of her, hugging her close.

She obediently raised her head only to draw in a quick breath. She almost forgot to let it out.

Her ceiling had completely disappeared, to be replaced with the most amazing glass dome.

"Good God," she sputtered, completely awestruck. "What happened to the roof?"

"It is fortunate that you live on the top floor of this building, Alana-love," grinned Sami. "It would have been more of a challenge if you'd been lower down. But never fear, this is a temporary creation—all can be returned to its normal state."

"And others will not see it from outside—it is in our dimension, not yours," added Hari reassuringly.

"But all this—this—*white*…" She looked at Hari and Sami, questions trembling on her lips.

"It is a special place for a special experience, Alana…but let's enjoy our meal first, and we will tell you all about it."

Hari led her unresistingly into the kitchen and seated her at the table, pulling a bottle of mineral water from the fridge and sliding it across to her.

Absently, she opened it and took a long drink.

"Okay guys, please explain to me why my room now looks like an ad for the cleaning power of Genie Sudso? Not that I object, mind you. I have thought of redecorating, but that was a little drastic."

"It is necessary to remove all external distractions for our next session, Alana," said Hari.

"Furniture is a distraction?"

"It might be. This way, the neutral surroundings will enhance the experience for you."

"And exactly what experience would that be?"

"How much do you know about Tantric Yoga?"

* * * * *

Alana gazed at the platter of fruit that Sami had just placed in the center of the table. The pleasing array of chopped papaya and mangoes mingled with the grapes and the shine of the mandarin oranges. But all these mouthwatering colors were wasted on Alana as she tried to pull some data on Tantric Yoga out of her befuddled brain.

"There's a musician who does it..." was the best she could come up with. "That's not much to start with, is it?" she winced.

Hari and Sami looked at each other and shook their heads. Sami filled his plate and began his meal, while Hari tilted his chair back on two legs, folded his hands across his marvelously sculpted abs and gazed thoughtfully at Alana.

"Hmmm. Where do I start? Tantra, Alana, is a very ancient perspective on life, which is probably something like five thousand years old. It holds everything, each and every aspect of creation, most sacred. The word 'Tantra' is from the Sanskrit, and can be translated as—um—expanding, spreading. Tantric beliefs include the concept of energies, which can be expanded and woven together. It's a very spiritual belief that is difficult to fully explain. It is very mystical in its acceptance of a kind of interconnectedness—a spiritual link, so to speak—between our universe and ourselves. Are you with me so far?"

"Yes, I think so. Where does the sex come in?"

Sami chuckled. "Don't like to waste time on preliminaries, do you?"

Alana blushed. "It's all your fault."

"That's all right, Alana-love. It would take much more time than we have to instruct you fully in the ways of Tantra—and you're right, Tantric yoga has become associated mostly with sex."

He leaned over and took a swig of Alana's water.

"The practitioners of Tantric yoga believe that sexual energy is one of the most fundamental—it is, after all, the process whereby life is created. So the aim of Tantric yoga is to release that sexual energy, blend it with that of your bedmate and experience a sexual release that is different from any you've experienced before. Simply put, the ability to have a Tantric orgasm is a liberating experience, and goes a long way toward releasing one's inhibitions and preconceived notions about one's sexual abilities."

Alana gaped at him.

"Wow."

Sami bit his lip. "It is really not that complicated, Alana," he said, trying not to laugh at her rather dubious expression.

"Well—it sounds good, but I've never been one for this new-age hippie kind of stuff, and the one time I took a Yoga course I wrenched my back."

Hari sat his chair up straight.

"Alana, give me your hands," he said, stretching his arms across the table.

She placed her hands in his palms. He closed his fingers, lightly holding hers.

"Now I want you to close your eyes and try to empty your mind—think of a deserted beach, a piece of black velvet cloth—anything simple and uncluttered." The warmth from his hands grew as he kept his clasp light but solid.

"I want you to be aware of your breathing—open your lips slightly—inhale through your nose and exhale through your lips. No..." He squeezed her fingers as she blew out a harsh breath.

"It should be a natural breathing rhythm—just in and out, nose and lips. Remember to focus on the simplicity within your mind,"

Alana focused, finding it easier than she thought to catch the rhythm.

"Good, that's good, Alana," said Hari quietly.

"Now I want you to remember an erotic experience— let's try our bath together. Do you remember that?"

Hari's voice soothed her with its rich cadence, and she smiled, eyes closed, remembering.

"Oh yessss..." she breathed.

"Now I want you to move your body a little, just rock back and forth in time with your breathing, can you do that?"

In answer to a little tug from Hari's fingers, Alana rocked forward and then back as he released her.

"Now as you rock back, I want you to clench your pubic muscles—then release them as you rock forward. Try now…" encouraged Hari.

It took a few tries, but eventually Alana got the hang of it, coordinating her breathing, her rocking and her clenching. Hari's fingers were still on hers, helping her keep a smooth rhythm and gentle movements—there was nothing overt here, it was so subtle that she could have been swaying to music.

Hari and Sami nodded to each other, but their actions went unnoticed by Alana. She had grasped the idea of the movements and was completely focused on what she was doing.

"That is excellent, Alana. Tell me, what are you feeling?"

"I'm feeling—I'm feeling very warm where your hands are holding mine, Hari, and I'm feeling a kind of fullness—um—it's very arousing—"

Her grip on Hari's fingers tightened.

"I'm thinking of Sami's mouth and lips and tongue on me while you touch me in— um—other places…"

Alana blushed slightly and her rocking became a little more rhythmic.

"Oh my—this is incredible—I feel—I feel…"

"What do you feel, Alana?" asked Hari, keeping his hands on hers as she started to breathe more quickly.

"I feel like I'm going to—going to—oh, God—I'm going to come!"

She gasped and threw her head back, squeezing Hari's fingers 'til they were bloodless. Her mouth opened in a silent scream and shivers racked her, finally leaving her drained and bowed, head resting on the table.

Her hands slid from Hari's.

"Holy cow."

* * * * *

"That was excellent, Alana." Hari beamed at her with pride.

"You said it," agreed Alana, blowing hair away from her forehead with a big whoosh. "And I don't feel tired, either."

"Tantric sex is energizing rather than depleting," added Sami. "You are feeling the effects of having tapped into the energies around you to have an orgasm. Wait 'til you have one with Hari."

Alana's jaw dropped as she considered the possibilities.

"But first, eat—the fruits are an excellent pre-Tantric meal. The papaya and the pineapple contain digestive enzymes which will aid in your digestion, thus freeing up your body's physical resources," said Sami, sounding like a nutrition class.

"The other fruits contain sugars and carbohydrates that are easily converted into energy that will help sustain you, and there is nothing here that will slow any of your body's processes down—you will be fully fueled for your journey."

"Um—if you say so," said Alana, tucking into a plate full of delicious fruit that Sami slid across in front of her.

"We will spend the afternoon in a restful fashion—both Sami and I would like to try our hand at your puzzles—we have some items which are similar in our quarters. Would this be a possibility?"

"Hari—you don't even need to ask. Of course, you may do whatever you like. Is there anything I should be doing to prepare for this—er—Tantric thingy?"

"You may rest, you may take a leisurely bath, you may read—all we ask is that you keep your activities tranquil so that the body and the mind may be fully relaxed by the time we begin. I will also tell you now that Sami will not be joining us for this experience—the presence of another would be too distracting."

"Oh, and you're not, I suppose," muttered Alana, enjoying the sensual picture Hari made as his hand idly stroked across his chest and flat nipple.

"Truth to tell, Alana, my decorating stint this morning has exhausted me. I will relish the chance to sleep for several hours and sort of recharge my energies. Having you in my arms at night can be disturbing on many levels…" Sami wiggled his brows playfully.

Alana sighed. If George could only manage that little maneuver.

Of course, having two lovely Djinns doing jigsaw puzzles on her coffee table wasn't the most restful thing in the world, mused Alana a few hours later.

Her heartbeat quickened just from watching them. Sami's golden silk hair fell onto his shoulders as he nibbled a finger and tried to fit the piece he was holding into an available slot.

Alana's clit twitched at the sight of his tongue as it swept across his lips.

Hari had secured his hair at the back of his neck with a loose tie. It was a flattering look, throwing his finely sculpted features into prominence and letting light flash from his dark eyes every now and again.

She started getting wet—just their presence was so sexually overwhelming.

"Alana, do you have a favorite novel?"

"Huh?"

"A book? Do you have a favorite book?"

Caught off-guard for a moment, she yanked her thoughts back from where they'd been. "Er—yeah—sure, why?"

"Does it have any sexual content?" Hari asked.

"A little, yeah…"

"Well, may I suggest you take that book and go have a nice long, soothing bath. You're getting too excited too soon. You need to relax. And make sure you skip the sexy bits." Hari grinned at her.

"How do you know? You guys have some kind of arousal antenna?"

Sami smiled. "We can smell you, Alana."

"Eeeuuuw. Gross."

"Not at all. The scent of your arousal is a very exciting thing. For lovemaking to be all that it can, the man should relish the aroma of his woman's body preparing itself for his loving."

"Oh. Well, when you put it like that, I suppose…" said Alana, still struggling with an assortment of issues, none of which were making much sense.

"I'd better go have that bath."

Chapter Twelve

The scent of Blue Lotus greeted Alana as she stepped out of the bathroom swathed in the long white silk robe she'd found hanging on the back of the door. One thing you could say for these guys—they certainly knew their fabrics.

The long, indulgent soak had relaxed her considerably. It was with a great deal of tactile pleasure that she allowed her fingers to drift over her hip and down her thigh, feeling the slick material gently cascade through her fingers.

The light was changing as the sun set, and she noticed that the candles had been lit. Hari walked in with a long container of matches.

Alana gaped. He was wearing a matching silk robe, only in black, and he looked like every hero from the cover of every romance novel she'd ever seen come to life— and he was in *her* bedroom. Thank you, Lord!

His hair fell loose over his shoulders and he smiled at her, adding to the devastation. My God, this man was about a thirty-eight on the sexual Richter scale.

He moved to the small braziers that stood between the candles and lit a match, touching it carefully to the contents. Soon a delicate smoke emerged, scented with cinnamon, vanilla, a touch of sage and the ever-present Blue Lotus. It was soothing, unusual, and Alana found herself lifting her head and sniffing at the air like a dog catching a strange scent.

Taking her by the shoulders, Hari led her to the soft animal skin rug. He stood her just about arms-length away from himself and pushed an errant lock of hair back behind her ear.

"We will start by clearing our thoughts, Alana-delight. As you did earlier, try and concentrate on something simple—an empty shore, plain fabric, an empty room— whatever relaxes and eases your mind. However, this time, see if you can do it with your eyes open—you may look into mine as a focus point if you care to."

She gazed into Hari's chocolate brown eyes as instructed, trying to clear the extraneous thoughts from her head. The incense was becoming a little stronger now, and she could swear she saw Hari's pupils dilate as he stared deeply into her eyes in return.

"Now take your hand and place it over my heart—just here," said Hari, helping her find the correct spot. She felt his warmth and the sturdy beat of his heart through the silk.

"And I shall do the same," he added.

His right hand reached to her breast, but lay just beneath, on her heart rather than her nipple. Drat.

"Focus, Alana," reprimanded Hari gently.

"I'm trying," she muttered, doing her level best to ignore the wonderfully firm muscle underneath her palm.

"We are going to try to feel the energies in our bodies—to tap into the life force flowing through us…" Hari's voice caressed nerves up and down Alana's spine.

"Imagine your hand passing through my skin, through my muscle into a place deep within me where there is a rushing and throbbing flow of energy circulating around my body—try to see it in your mind and feel it in your hand. I shall do the same."

Alana found she needed to close her eyes to concentrate, and as she did, the heat beneath her palm increased.

She could almost see Hari as a silhouette, black and gold, glittering around the edges like an x-ray. The pulsating current under her hand took on a life of its own and she jumped as she felt a tingle, not unlike an electric shock. She pulled her hand away with a gasp, realizing that Hari's palm was burning into her skin beneath her breast.

Hari backed away, a pleased smile on his face.

"You were almost there, Alana. That is very good indeed for a first attempt."

She smiled back, feeling a little lightheaded, although whether that was a result of her brush with Hari's life force or the incense that she was inhaling, she couldn't tell.

"Now we have sensed our inner energies, it is time to stimulate our auras."

He reached forward and loosened the tie on Alana's robe, allowing it to fall open. He bent his head slightly and raised one brow, indicating that she should do the same. With fingers that only trembled a little, Alana leaned over and freed his robe.

It hung like a black veil down either side of his massive chest, throwing his abs into shadow and revealing his erection, which was impressive, to say the least.

Alana licked her lips.

"Now I want you to move your hands around my body without actually touching me—you'll be moving your hands through my aura. Concentrate on keeping your mind empty of distractions, and tell me what you feel," said Hari, as he stepped a little closer.

Alana followed his instructions, refusing to allow the sight of this magnificent, almost-nude male to distract her. Yeah, right. Sighing, Alana started over again.

Hari's movements mirrored hers, his large hands sweeping slowly across her shoulders and down her sides, never touching, but close enough that she could feel the warmth emanating from his palms.

She ran her hand down his naked chest and gasped as she felt — something.

"What, Alana-love?"

"I — it felt as though — like I was swirling my hand through lukewarm water — kind of there, but not..." she stuttered, trying to explain the unexplainable.

Hari smiled.

"Now remove my robe — push it off my shoulders..." he ordered, as his hands brushed the silk off her body.

Naked, they faced each other.

"Continue your movements, Alana," encouraged Hari softly.

This time, there was no doubt in Alana's mind. Her hands passed close to Hari's body and tingled. It was as if there was a little force field there — and when she moved lower to his hips and abdomen, she wouldn't have been surprised to see sparks.

"Our sexual energies are being enhanced, Alana-mine," whispered Hari. "Can you feel it?"

She wasn't quite sure what she was feeling. Her head was spinning ever so slightly. Both her hands were now tingling as they moved around Hari, and she was so focused on her exercise that she didn't realize that darkness had completely fallen. The room was lit only by the candles, which sent their flickering rays dimly through the swirl of incense.

"Come, Alana, we will progress…"

Hari took her hand away from his navel and pulled her toward the futon and two large cushions.

She was almost angry with him for interrupting her meditations—she wanted to feel more of his energy tickling her fingertips.

Hari chuckled.

"There is much more, Alana, trust me."

He knelt, then sat on the cushion in the traditional meditative position, thighs splayed wide and ankles crossed. He pulled the other pillow between his legs and patted it.

"Sit here, Alana, as I am sitting, with your legs over mine," he held her hand firmly as she swayed slightly and then settled into his lap as he had directed.

"Cross your ankles behind me—good."

Alana realized that her pussy was opened wide to his gaze. She looked down to see his cock inches from her body and her juices moistening her already glistening labia.

"Alana—I need you to concentrate on my eyes, my love…"

He had to be kidding, right?

But he wasn't. "Alana, look into my eyes—it is important that we hold each other's gaze from now on. It is another in the connections between us that we are going to explore. Place your hand back on my chest—reactivate your contact with my *chi*—my life force."

His hand touched her skin again, scorching her flesh.

This time, she willingly pressed against him, keeping her eyes fixed on his. Concentrating, she cleared her mind, and allowed the hot, tingly sensation into her hand and up her arm.

"Good, that is very good," quietly encouraged Hari.

"Keep looking into my eyes—see my desire for you as it grows stronger," he murmured.

Alana heard a rhythmic drumbeat in her mind and realized it was her heart—or was it Hari's? She couldn't tell—they were beating in synchronized time with each other.

"Feel our energies weaving together, Alana, deepening, merging—I am coming into you and you are coming into me."

She smiled dreamily into his eyes, watching his pupils as they dilated with pleasure. The energies that surrounded her hand were spreading out—she wondered if her hair was standing on end like it did in those static electricity displays.

"Feel the forces taking over more and more of your body, my delight," crooned Hari. "The flow is dropping, down and down to your pleasure centers, to your yin and my yang, preparing for the moment when we shall truly blend our flow…"

Alana lost herself in Hari's eyes—dark pools of mystery, reflecting her nude body back at her, shining in the soft candlelight.

She pulled in a quick breath as Hari's cock flickered against her.

"Don't look away, Alana. I am going to close the circle between us…" And he scooted forward very slightly to rest the head of his cock at her entrance.

She sighed in delight.

"Oh God, Hari, that feels so good—so hot…" she breathed.

"Keep your hand on my body—feel our energies as I feel yours. Now we are joined and our energies are close to becoming one…"

Alana licked lips that had suddenly gone dry.

"Can you feel my energies, love, can you feel the beat of my life force? I can feel yours." His eyes devoured her.

Lost in sensation, she concentrated, realizing that she could indeed feel every throb of his huge cock as it rested on her swollen folds. Her clit pulsed in time with his heartbeat.

He pulled her closer and entered her until the flared head of his cock was snuggled tightly into her cunt.

"You may remove your hand from my chest now, Alana—we are truly joined…" breathed Hari, eyes black with desire.

Alana scarcely blinked as she eased her hand from his chest and rested her arms on his shoulders.

"Mmmm…" she said dreamily, content with the sensation of his energies flowing into her and becoming one with her.

Hari moved even closer. Now almost all his cock was buried within her and his heat spread up through her body, making every nerve tingle. Her nipples budded and tightened, and she gasped as she felt his chest hairs lightly caress them. Their eyes never broke contact.

"Now we move," whispered Hari.

His hands clasped her buttocks gently, and he rocked forward, pushing himself deep inside her.

Then he pulled back, encouraging her to follow his movements. Alana let out a groaning sigh of delight.

"Oh. My. God."

Her world was tipped upside down. She felt as if they were three feet off the pillows, hell—they could have been orbiting Saturn for all she knew. Dancing particles of energy flickered over her sensitized skin and her pussy wept for joy as Hari continued his rhythmic rocking—in and out.

Her cunt spasmed once, and again, then spasmed in time with the plunging of Hari's cock.

A sound of ecstasy was wrung out of Hari, but still they gazed deep into each other's eyes.

They rocked and gazed, bodies now so close together that the slightest breath either of them took was felt by the other.

They shared heartbeats, their juices mingled into one brilliant flow, and their eyes remained fixed on each other.

Hari pulled Alana to him that final inch and his body continued to rock, abrading her clit now as he did so.

Gently he eased her up to the next level—her spasms were becoming more intense —she realized she was having little orgasms and her whole body took on a level of awareness she'd never have believed possible.

She felt Hari's cock throbbing and swelling even more inside her—the feeling of exquisite fullness emphasized by the gentle continuous rocking and the sensual liberation of watching him as he remained buried inside her body.

His eyes reflected his passion, almost completely black now — the pupils had expanded to obliterate the brown iris. Sweat was breaking out on his brow, and she knew they had to be close to...something.

"Let your energies release, Alana, let my cock take your life force — share with me..."

The rocking continued, and gradually Alana felt a tension rise within her body. It started in her cunt, ran through her clit and erupted up, up toward her shoulders and her neck.

She knew her eyes must be widening at this amazing sensation — her internal muscles were tightening around Hari's cock and she could smell the mixture of sweat and their sexual juices over the incense.

Every single iota of awareness she possessed crystallized into blinding focus as an enormous rush of power gushed through her body and blew the top of her head off. For the first time she broke away from Hari's gaze as her head fell back, her neck muscles tensed and she shrieked silently, riding out an orgasm that threatened to completely pulverize her intestines.

Hari was with her. Straining, he bent his head and tucked it into her neck, ramming himself as far into her contracting channel as he could and allowing the intense muscle contractions to bring him to his climax. He came with a shout, pumping for endless eons into Alana.

Wisps of blue fog danced up from where they were joined, catching the candlelight like iridescent starlight captured by the moment.

They stilled, holding each other, neither willing to break the spell that held them, joined them and made them one.

Chapter Thirteen

"Holy shit," muttered Alana from the depths of the futon.

"That about sums it up, yeah," groaned Hari, face down and sprawled next to her.

"That was…that was completely…Tantric."

"Yeah."

"Hari?"

"Mmm?"

Alana stroked her hand lovingly over Hari's firm buttocks, loving the feeling of the tender flesh responding to her movements.

"Does this happen every time a couple gets Tantricized, or whatever you call it?"

Hari turned his head fully toward her, snuggling a little so that she could reach both buns. He grinned.

"Nope."

"No?"

"Uh uh."

"So what just happened…between us, I mean…that wasn't a normal Tantric orgasm?"

"Well, for starters I don't think there is such a thing as a *normal* Tantric orgasm— it's different for everybody. But a general train of thought is that at least one the partners has to be a skilled practitioner of various forms of yoga, including the Tantric forms, for this to be a successful experience."

Her fingers danced along the cleft of his buttocks and she noticed his fragile hairs stiffening as she gave him goosebumps.

"So, I may never have another orgasm like that without you, is that what you're saying?"

Hari caught her wandering hand and brought it to his lips.

"Alana-love, there are many wonderful experiences lying ahead of you, and some of them may indeed involve the Tantra—it depends. Are you interested in learning the practice perhaps? Or maybe a future partner will be an adherent. The possibilities are endless. My participation is unnecessary."

"Oh, Hari," she sighed, snuggling toward him.

He pulled her head onto his shoulder and tucked her body close to his.

"Rest now, Alana, worry in the morning if you must, but for now, let your body and your mind settle and become comfortable with your new knowledge of yourself and the world around you."

She gazed through the glass dome at the night sky, peppered with stars.

Hari was right. She had felt the touch of something greater than herself, some kind of energy that had nothing to do with power plants and everything to do with nature. It was a humbling experience, and trying to consider all the implications seemed an impossible task right at that moment.

Her eyelids drooped, and, lulled by the sound of Hari's heartbeat, she slid rapidly into sleep.

Hari smiled, dropped a kiss on the top of her head and closed his eyes.

* * * * *

Alana giggled at the puppies in her arms. There were two adorable, soft and cuddly pups, and she was cradling them and crooning to them as they wriggled and writhed against her. Then they started licking her.

She laughed aloud at the tickling sensation of their tongues, then gasped as their tongues flickered over her nipples—she realized she was quite naked. Why was she holding puppies when she had no clothes on? Were they teething? What if they peed? What if—

She opened her eyes to see two heads close together over her breasts, each gently suckling a nipple.

"Jeez, guys—you're a hell of an alarm clock," she yawned, stretching her arms above her head.

Hari and Sami raised their heads and gave her almost-identical smiles then returned to their task—bringing her breasts awake to the point of exquisite sensation.

They were doing a damn fine job.

She dropped her arms and rested them on warm solid shoulders. The affection she felt for these two beings swelled in her heart and she caressed the two heads, sliding her fingers through their hair.

They were devoted to her—her pleasure, her comfort, how could she ever manage a normal life, having known this kind of experience? Hallucination though it might be, it was going to ruin her. And it was going to rip her heart out when the time came for them to leave.

A sob hiccupped its way into her throat, and she burst into tears.

"Alana-love—" said Hari in a panicked voice.

"What is it, my delight..." murmured Sami, brushing her hair away from her face and watching her tears fall in horror.

"Tell us, Alana—please—are you in pain? Did we hurt you? What is it?"

Both Hari and Sami petted and patted and stroked her—a portion of Alana's mind realized she was seeing an example of the power of tears to reduce a man to a nervous wreck.

"I don't want to have to say goodbye to you guys— my life will NEVER be the same," she wailed.

"Oh, Alana," said Sami hugging her tight. "Is that all?"

"All? You think that's all? That I can spend timeless millennia fucking around with you two and treat it as something casual?" Alana sat up, irate. "And don't think you can distract me, Hari, because it won't work this time..."

Hari looked down at his hand, which was gently circling her clit. He seemed surprised, almost as if he had no idea what his fingers were doing down there.

"Sorry," he muttered, giving her a little reassuring tweak.

She ignored the thrill that jolted her.

"Alana-love, after the time we have spent together, do you really think we would allow you the pain of such a parting?"

Alana sniffed.

Hari materialized a box of tissues.

"Jeez, where were you when I ran out of toilet paper the other day," grumbled Alana.

"Blow your nose, delight. Tears in the morning should be of ecstasy, not sadness."

"The worries you have are groundless, Alana — our separation is inevitable, but we can assure you that you will not suffer because of it. Perhaps now you understand why the Djinns are not allowed to retain memories of their students. We would suffer this anguish every time an assignment concluded," said Sami.

Alana sighed.

"I suppose you'll make me forget too?"

"You will have memories, Alana. There would be no point in this entire project if you were to have the recollection erased at the end, would there?"

"No…"

"But what you will remember is what you learned with us — our actual selves will be as a distant memory of a much-loved story. The secrets of your womanhood that we have helped you uncover will remain."

"The secrets of my womanhood…" mused Alana. "I'm still not sure if I have any…"

Sami laughed. "Alana, Alana. You have already learned much — you are understanding that the real secret of sexuality lies not in here— " he touched her pussy, " — or here— " he touched her forehead, " —but here." His hand lay over her heart.

"You are learning that your heart will lead you to the right lover. When your heart is involved, the rest, including the sex, comes naturally."

"Terrific, eye-rolling, heel-thumping sex, like I'm having with you guys?"

"Yep."

"Oh." Alana blew her nose.

"And speaking of terrific, eye-rolling, heel-thumping sex, we need to see about having some..." Hari gave her breast a last swipe of his tongue and rolled off the bed, while Alana admired his really fine ass—that would be *really* fine—Alana's mind added the capitals as she observed the firm, deliciously rounded and slightly tanned cheeks and the way they flowed into the strong thigh muscles below. Even the indentation at the base of his spine cried out for the touch of fingers or lips—or even a gentle bite or two.

Sami grinned as he watched Alana's expression.

"Down, girl."

Alana jumped guiltily and turned to Sami. She noticed that his cock was, as always, beautifully erect and resting on her thigh. She stroked it gently and watched as it twitched and writhed a little under her touch.

"Hey, you can't blame a girl for enjoying the scenery, can you?" She flicked her fingers under the head and heard Sami's breath as it was quickly indrawn.

"Between the two of you, I feel like I'm in the Testosterone Louvre. Art is everywhere I look."

Sami's eyes were slightly glazed as she gave his cock a little tug.

Hari snorted. "Alana—you are too generous with your praise. Now put Sami down and go have breakfast, or shower or something, because he and I have a little housekeeping to do and a few things to plan."

"Oh, what things?" asked Alana, giving Sami's cock an absent pat.

"Things like a special graduation for you, perhaps."

"Oh?"

"Yep."

"Like what?"

"Can't tell. You'll find out. Now scoot—we have chores."

Alana scooted.

* * * * *

It was a long and very refreshing shower—Alana had grabbed a cup of Sami's wonderful coffee to take in with her, and between the caffeine, the water, and her own practical nature, she felt able to take on anything. So what if she was eventually going to have to return to reality—it hadn't happened yet, and to judge by the gleam in her Djinns' eyes, there was more to come. She meant to enjoy every second of it.

Of course, once again she found herself missing her clothing. Sighing she grabbed a towel and strode out into the Sultan's harem.

No—wait—this was her bedroom. Oh God—Sami, the patron Djinn of interior design, had been at it again.

The dome was gone, replaced by a satin ceiling and wall hangings in the richest jewel colors she could ever remember seeing. A gorgeous oriental rug caressed her toes—the antiques lover in her drooled and gave up trying to guess its origin—it was simply magnificent.

The bed was at least a foot higher than her own—she'd need a running start to get into it, she thought with a little giggle. Soft sheers in matching tones of crimson, emerald and sapphire blue were twisted at the corners, giving the illusion of a four-poster. Pillows were casually tossed around, overstuffed and heavily embroidered in gold designs. All that was missing was the camel, some sand, and maybe the Sheik. But no, there he was.

Hari stood looking at her with a glint of desire in his eyes.

Alana's jaw dropped as she took in his costume. A brief vest covered his shoulders and stopped way north of his navel. Of some rich emerald green fabric, it glittered with thousands of little sparkles — tiny jewels stitched into the embroidered design. A low-slung belt circled his hips, made from the same fabric and with the same jeweled embroidery. His pants were sheer and were clearly purchased from the reduced for clearance camel train — they were missing an important part — the entire front and back.

"My God — I didn't know they made chaps back in the days of the harem."

Hari's lips twitched once.

"We find it acceptable to take ideas from whatever time we visit and adapt them for our own ends," he announced, folding his hands across his chest and looking so much like the lead in some porno flick like *Triple X Genies — Desert Hotties,* that Alana found it very hard to stifle a giggle.

"Well — it's very nice, Hari," she said carefully. "Um — do I get to wear anything?"

"Oh — sorry — yes — we were rather busy finishing this up..." He absently waved his hand and Alana found herself in two tissues and a scarf. Or what felt like two tissues and a scarf.

A sheer vest draped her shoulders, ending just above the lower curve of her breasts. It was so sheer that one good sneeze would have blown holes in it. There were some little sequins glittering on the hem and it was totally see-through.

Her hips were swathed in a strip of silk. It knotted on one hip and didn't quite cover the neatly trimmed curls between her thighs.

"Well, it could be worse, I suppose. At least they didn't have thongs in the harem…"

Sami entered the room and Alana's eyes widened. He was wearing an identical outfit to Hari, but his was in the deepest of royal blues. He was carrying a small table, which he stood next to the bed.

Curiosity drove Alana over to see what was on it.

There was a silken cord with a huge tassel and some strangely shaped objects — the function of which she could only guess at.

Sami leapt onto the bed and threw himself back against the cushions. His cock readied itself, resting against his hard abdomen.

He smiled. A very wicked smile.

Hari crossed to Alana's side.

"You are now in the presence of the Mighty Sheik. Alana, on your knees — he will be judging your suitability for his harem from this point on." Hari's hand pressed her down and she knelt on the soft rug.

"Excellency, this unworthy woman begs permission to convince you of her desire to become one with your Mightiness…"

Alana squirmed at the "unworthy" bit. "Just a minute…" she hissed.

"It's a fantasy, Alana, hush up…"

Muttering, she subsided.

Sami raised his head slightly.

"She may approach. You may use her as you will, Seneschal—I shall judge her performance accordingly."

"Your graciousness is as boundless as the skies, as deep as the widest sea, as—"

"Yeah, yeah, move it along, will you? My knees are cramping here," hissed Alana, still a tad pissed at the "unworthy" comment.

Hari snickered, but raised her from the floor.

"Let me see her," said Sami, reclining comfortably on one arm.

Hari ripped the sheer bodice away and flipped her scarf down to her toes. She stood there, nude, while Sami's eyes feasted on her.

Amazingly, she felt a blush start in her cheeks and sweep down across her breasts. This was Sami, for heaven's sake. He knew her better and more intimately than her gynecologist. Why was she blushing?

"Is her cunt wet?" asked Sami.

"Shall I check, Your Worship?"

Sami nodded once.

Hari's hand passed behind her and through her legs, cupping her mound. She knew she was dripping her hot juices all over him.

"She is wet, Highness," said Hari, bringing his hand to his lips and sucking his fingers with evident pleasure.

"We are pleased. Bring her closer for my delectation. Oh—and I have a new book—I may read some instructions from time to time." Sami (excuse me, the Grand Sheik) held up a book with a heavily ornamented cover. The writing was unfamiliar to her.

"What's that?" she whispered to Hari.

"Ever hear of the Kama Sutra?"

She gulped.

"Come nearer, Flower of the Desert," said Sami.

Trying not to giggle, Alana moved to the very edge of the bed. Sami reached out and stroked her breasts, pulling and teasing her nipples into hard buds.

She groaned.

'We shall begin with 'Nimitta' — the touching."

Hari smiled. "Oh goody." That got him a frown from Sami, who was really getting into his role as Sheik.

"Woman, take this man's cock into your hands. You will place your mouth just on its tip—kiss it gently."

Alana knelt by the bed and glanced up at Hari. He was hard as a rock and his expression was a blend of eagerness and, surprisingly, nerves.

It was no hardship to reach out and lovingly cradle his cock in her hand. She followed Sami's directions and fluttered small kisses around the tip. Sami turned a page.

"Put your lips around the head and use them to pull and press the skin—gently."

"Bahiha-samdansha?" asked Hari over Alana's ministrations.

Sami nodded, grinning at Hari.

"Woman, feel the head of his cock with your tongue — find the tip and the underside — concentrate the movements of your tongue in those places while you pull him from between your lips and then slide him back in."

Alana did her best to follow instructions — finding to her surprise that it was arousing to her, and a lot more fun than she'd been led to believe. Oral sex had never been on her list of fun activities, but maybe it was time to rethink her list. Her hand came up to grip his cock at the base, and she timed the movements of her head to an accompanying squeeze and pull of her fingers.

Hari's buttocks tightened and he stifled a moan.

"Alana — up on the bed here, now," Sami ordered, dropping the book off the side of the bed.

Releasing Hari with a slurp, Alana looked up, slightly dazed.

Sami patted the bed.

"I want you up here on your stomach. Climb up…" He held out his hand and half-pulled her up, moving his legs to make room for her.

"Now lie on your stomach with your head almost falling off the edge. Hari?"

Hari moved up to Alana's face, cock glistening from her attentions. A drop of moisture eased from the tiny slit in the head.

"Continue, Alana. Remember to relax all your muscles and welcome Hari into your body," said Sami, beginning a rhythmic stroke of Alana's buttocks. She squirmed slightly as Hari's cock thrust into her mouth.

"Easy, Alana-love, relax," murmured Hari, easing back, then moving forward again.

Her tongue sought, and found, the super-sensitive spot underneath the ridged head of Hari's cock and his indrawn breath spurred her on. She tightened her lips and created even more suction, pulling the sensitive skin as she moved her mouth on him. Unable to stop herself, one hand reached out to gently touch Hari's balls. He groaned.

Something cool and slick caressed her buttocks — Sami was rubbing some kind of lotion on her, distracting her. Her muscles relaxed as Sami's hand smoothed her skin, then tensed again as she felt her cheeks being eased apart and more lotion being poured.

God — it felt so — so — *wild*…

Her clit was burning and her breasts were pebbled hard as the slight movements both Hari and Sami were making served to slide her back and forth across the satin spread. The slick friction of the satin matched the slick slide of her lips over and around Hari's cock — she flicked the very tip with her tongue and brought another moan to Hari's throat.

She felt something hard ease between her buttocks — it was cool and slippery, and *ohmigod* it was going up her ass. She clenched in reflex, drawing a yelp from Hari.

"Relax, Alana, this is a simple toy. Enjoy the sensation," whispered Sami, as he continued to press the whatever-it-was past her ring of tight muscles.

And the sensation was quite amazing. She felt each subtle move in the delicate tissues — it was arousing in a different kind of way, she couldn't have described it if her life depended on it.

Her internal muscles clamped at the strange intrusion, and she was so focused that she didn't realize that Hari was practically down her throat.

Her hands were clenching his buttocks, she was probably leaving fingernail imprints on his butt, and he was quietly panting with pleasure as he worked himself in her mouth.

"Alana—listen carefully to me. Take one hand and place it just behind Hari's balls."

Hari moved his legs apart slightly, and Alana struggled to bring her thoughts into line and do what she'd been told.

"Press two fingers up into his body, gently but firmly. Do you understand?"

Alana grunted around Hari's cock.

Each movement made her aware of the strangeness penetrating her anus, and she was unbelievably turned on by this unusual invasion of her body. She found herself pressing two fingers up into Hari's flesh.

He sighed as his cock flexed—once—twice, and touched the back of her throat.

"Keep up the pressure, Alana, you're doing great," encouraged the Sheik. His hands were still stroking her buttocks, giving a quick touch or turn to the toy in between her cheeks to let her know it was still there.

"Yessssss," breathed Hari, after a giant twitch.

He withdrew from her mouth and she eased her fingers away from his balls.

That's odd, thought Alana—no fog.

Hari smiled. "Your fingers were pressing on a most delicate spot, Alana, you kept me from ejaculating, yet I enjoyed a climax. You did very well." He lowered his head and kissed her nose.

"Why am I on my stomach?" she asked.

"Your mouth and throat are most nearly aligned in this position, Alana-love," answered Sami, still rubbing her bottom gently. "It minimizes the gag reflex and maximizes the pleasure for both."

"Aaaah…" she breathed as he gave his toy a quick swirl. "Now, about that toy — "

"You mean this toy?" laughed Sami, easing it out and pushing it back in again.

"Ooooh yesssss… *That* toy," sighed Alana. "What part of the camel is that?"

"Camel? That's not anything to do with a camel — that's a butt plug," said Sami.

"Oh jeez. Guys. Be a bit more creative, will you?"

Alana gasped as Sami withdrew the plug and tossed it over the side of the bed.

"You want creative, wench?" he asked, resuming his role as Sheik. "I think we can oblige."

Chapter Fourteen

Alana found herself rolled onto her back by Sami's strong hands, and spread-eagled over the bed. Hari had changed sides, and was gripping her ankles, pulling her until her legs dangled over the side. He pushed her thighs wide, exposing her glistening and swollen labia to his gaze.

He licked his lips.

Sami slid around her, running his tongue in and out of her ear and down her neck. She tossed her head and realized Sami was holding her arms firmly pressed against the softness of the bed.

She was trapped. Oh—this was quite terrible. So terrible she'd probably have to try and get away in about a year or two.

Sami's head dipped to her nipple and he pulled it briskly into his mouth, wrapping his tongue around it as he suckled strongly.

Alana writhed at the pleasure/pain.

Hari slid his arms under her legs and raised them, placing her heels on his shoulders. He stood straight between her outspread thighs, his cock erect and ready—it needed little more than a touch to send it ramming into her hot and ready channel.

Alana groaned as Hari plunged deep.

"Watch, Alana," whispered Sami, raising her head with his arm.

"Watch as Hari fucks you — *this* is the elemental experience — the function of a man and a woman and their bodies — see how well they fit..."

Incredibly, Alana watched, seeing Hari's cock as it withdrew almost to the head, shining with her juices and then slammed back into her so thoroughly that their pubic hair meshed.

Hari moved his hands and pulled her swollen lips apart.

"See how your clit is so anxious for Hari's touch, Alana?"

Sami helped her rise even more.

"See your pearl pushing out of your pussy? See how it begs to be caressed and licked and sucked? How it trembles for a passing blow from Hari's cock?"

She felt, more than saw, the air passing over her aroused clit, the draft generated by Hari as he enthusiastically and rhythmically fucked her blind.

Her nipples beaded even more, and Sami tweaked and twirled them even while he too watched Hari's cock.

"Oh God...Hari...Sami..." gasped Alana, feeling the telltale tingle of an oncoming orgasm.

They froze.

"Oh nooooo," shrieked Alana, throbbing with need.

"Wait, Alana-delight, there is much time yet..." soothed Sami, placing little nipping kisses over her shoulders and neck.

"There is no rush, love," added Hari, his cock just lying in Alana's cunt, resting comfortably in the silk of her body. "That was just the beginning."

He slid out of her slowly, allowing his cock to spread her juices all over her aroused pussy.

Then he lowered her legs, one to dangle freely, the other he bent at the knee and pushed to the side. She was more exposed than ever.

Hari plunged in to her sensitive tissues once again, making Alana shudder with sexual arousal.

In this position, her clit got more stimulation from Hari's body as he began his thrusting slowly, each movement heightening the sensations that were making her shiver and shake.

Sami fondled, caressed and played with her breasts, his obvious interest in Hari's technique exciting Alana even more. It was almost voyeuristic, very erotic and just plain weird, but she was loving every minute of it.

Once again, Hari seemed to sense Alana's orgasm as it began to build, and once again, to her immense frustration, they both eased back and allowed her to come down a little.

Sami pushed her shoulders and flipped her onto her stomach, while Hari kept her one leg bent beneath her. She felt stretched, exposed, and not unlike an erotic etching. Her juices ran freely down her leg—Hari caught them with his hand and smoothed them over and around her buttocks, allowing the cool air on wet flesh to add to her arousal.

Then he plunged back in.

Sami moved his head close to hers, finding her lips and forcing his tongue within. His kiss was intense, his tongue once again echoing the rhythm of Hari's cock and sending vibrations throughout her body.

She could feel Hari's balls slapping against her as he fucked her, his hands sometimes squeezing her cheeks, and other times separating them so that he could run a fingertip down her cleft.

Alana was strung tight on a web of unfulfilled desire. Her ears were humming, her body throbbing, and when Sami reached beneath her for her nipple without breaking his kiss she thought that she was finally going to make it.

And Hari did. A long and loud groan, accompanied by a violent shudder, announced that Hari had come. But Sami refused to allow Alana the same release, stroking her tongue gently with his, and squeezing her breasts. Neither Hari nor Sami touched her poor, aching, screaming clit.

"OhGodOhGodOhGod…" she chanted, thinking that it was quite possible she'd be the first woman to succumb to unfulfilled orgasm-itis.

"Yes, Alana—it's your turn now," growled Sami.

He pulled her up, waved away some lingering blue fog, moved so that he sat on the edge of the bed and swung her astride him. Her knees rested on either side of his hips and he grabbed his cock with his hand to guide it into Alana's aching cunt.

"Oh Sami…yesssssss…" she hissed as his huge length slid home into her body.

Hari moved between Sami's thighs and pressed his body to Alana's back.

"This is it, Alana…this is for you, and for us, and for the woman you have become…" he whispered into her ear.

His hands smoothed up and down her back, and he moistened her skin with more lotion. She felt him spread her cheeks and lubricate her tight anus.

"Oh Hari—I've never...I don't know if this is such a good idea," she sputtered nervously.

"Alana," said Sami. "Look into my eyes. See the love we bear for you. We will never, ever hurt you."

Alana gazed into the glittering blue depths that were so near, and saw a mixture of desire, need and—yes—love. Her body relaxed and she smiled tentatively.

Sami moved his hips slightly and slid his hand between them to her clit.

Hari tucked himself between her cheeks.

Sami's gentle stroking and circling were echoed as he once again touched his mouth to hers and began his sensuous kiss.

Hari pressed himself against Alana's anus, stroking cool moisture over and around the tight rose, never going too far but always going a little further.

One hand slid around her body to her breast, and he cupped it, presenting it to Sami for attention.

"I have come once already, Alana," his deep voice murmured into her neck. "My cock is not as large as it might have been. All you have to do is relax—you can take me inside you."

The touches of Sami's hands and mouth, along with Hari's whispers and fondles, were advancing Alana's arousal to a whole new level.

Her clit was covered in her own juices and sliding between Sami's fingers as his lips suckled and teased her nipple.

Hari's hand was lifting her breast higher, forcing her back to straighten as he rubbed himself over her cleft.

She moaned and pushed her clit into Sami's fingers, seeking more stimulation.

He sucked her nipple fiercely against the roof of his mouth, following that with little nips that were just short of painful.

Suddenly, with an odd little stinging feeling, Hari pushed himself past her barrier and into her virgin ass.

She was astonished at the feeling of both cocks inside her, and froze for a few seconds.

"Oh. My. Sweet. God," she breathed, unable to focus and staring inwards at what was happening to her.

Sami moved slightly, and Hari's body responded.

Good lord, Hari could feel Sami's cock through the thin membrane that separated them. She felt the heat of Hari's body against her back as he slid in a little more.

Sami panted and moaned as Hari moved.

"You two can feel — I can feel — you're both almost — " she stuttered, searching vainly for words to explain the unexplainable.

"Alana," whispered Hari. "Do not move. This sensation is so exquisite for both of us that it must be savored."

"I will touch you and bring you to orgasm now, Alana, but we do not wish to hurt you, so please try to stay still," added Sami, bringing both hands down to her pussy.

Stay still? Stuffed full of genie cock and microseconds away from an end-of-the-world orgasm and he said stay still?

Sami's fingers parted her swollen labia and eased even more of her clit from beneath its protective hood. He was buried so far inside her that their bodies were slammed tight and it was a matter of less than an inch for him to rub himself against her.

Slowly and surely, a tremendous orgasm started. Her buttocks tingled and she could almost feel the blood rushing to her tissues.

Sami's abrading caress continued bringing her up and up until she knew she couldn't stand it any more.

Then…it happened. Alana screamed as wave upon wave of shattering spasms rocked her body.

Hari yelled with pleasure and Sami sobbed out a breath as her violent contractions clamped down on their cocks.

Unwilling to let it go, Sami continued his movements, and Alana's eyes flew open as she realized it wasn't over.

Hari pushed in even more and Sami bit down on her nipple. Another stronger pulse hit her, starting low on her spine and exploding through every nerve ending. Gasping and voiceless, Alana closed her eyes and rode out the storm, unable to believe that wave after wave of orgasms were sweeping through her. Sami released her breast, threw his head back and yelled, his cock pumping and throbbing inside Alana and bringing on another orgasm.

Hari, helpless against the twin onslaughts of Sami's and Alana's orgasms, gave up the fight and let himself come again, pressing Alana's shoulders back against his chest as he too, trembled with the force of his climax.

They held each other tight as the blue fog seeped from Alana's body to mix with the sweat, the lotion and the sex juices that were now liberally splattered everywhere.

It was too much for Alana. She leaned her head back against Hari, locked her arms around Sami's neck and passed out.

* * * * *

Thousands of years later, Alana struggled back to consciousness. Well, it felt like it could have been thousands of years—although more practically, it was probably only minutes.

She was lying flat on her back between two completely dead-to-the-world genies. The air above the bed was thick with blue fog, and tendrils were still swirling from her pussy. She stretched gently, and surprised herself with a little fart. Blue fog coiled upwards.

"Oh swell. Now *I'm* doing it too…" she muttered, rolling to the side and farting fog once more.

She buried her blushing face in the pillow as a snicker of laughter emerged from Hari's side of the bed.

"Don't you dare laugh at me," she mumbled into the silk. "It's your fault I'm full of fog."

Hari's rich laugh woke Sami.

"Our delight is finding that she can call the camels with blue fog, my brother…"

"Call the camels?"

"Sometimes the sound of escaping gas can sound like the grunt of a camel—we refer to it as 'calling the camels'," explained Hari, following it up with a rather boisterous demonstration of his own.

Not to be outdone, Sami moved slightly and contributed another camel call.

"Okay…guys…thank you. I get the point. Just so that you know—it's not considered polite to do that in mixed company."

Alana sat up and tried to look severe, failing entirely as another small fart exploded from her ass and belched blue fog up her back.

There was dead silence for a moment, and then all three burst into laughter, holding each other and giggling until the tears were running down Alana's face, and Hari and Sami were clasping their ribs in pain.

They would stop for a moment, then one would catch the eye of the others and they would start anew. Just when she thought they were getting their wits back, Alana lost the battle of the clenched cheeks and popped out another small blue cloud.

That was all it took—hysteria ruled again.

By the time they had actually relaxed enough to enjoy rational conversation, Alana felt it was time for a few answers.

"So guys—did I make the Harem of Sheik Sami, here?"

She leaned over and kissed him soundly on the lips.

"Mmmm…" said Sami. "Alana-love, you kicked every other concubine firmly out on their asses."

"It was something else, Alana," added Hari, who then got his own mouth soundly kissed in gratitude.

Alana struggled up onto the pillows and put her arms around their shoulders, bringing them in close to her body. It felt natural, warm, and comforting—like being snuggled in a basket of puppies.

"Why me, guys?"

"What do you mean, dear delight?"

"Why did you pick me? Why was I the one allowed to buy your vessel?"

Chapter Fifteen

"In truth, we do not know, Alana," Hari answered her question.

"The Guardian is the one who handles our assignments—but we can tell you that there is always a good reason for his choices. Perhaps it is that you will bear a child someday who is destined for great achievements?"

Alana pondered this statement.

"Or maybe you will be able to provide love and satisfaction to a man who will very much need what you can give him now," added Sami.

"There are as many reasons as stars in the sky, Alana-delight," murmured Hari, circling her nipple delicately with his finger.

"But whatever they are, we are certainly glad that the Guardian sent us to you."

"So, do I graduate? Was that my final exam, so to speak?" asked Alana, dreading the answer.

"Well, yes and no," said Sami, grinning.

"In ordinary circumstances, your achievements would have guaranteed your graduation—we'd have a small ceremony and that would be it."

"But? I sense a definite 'but?' there, Sami," stated Alana, poking him in the chest. She nearly bent her finger backwards.

"We—" Sami nodded across her at Hari, who'd replaced his finger with his tongue and was doing lovely playful things to her nipple, "...we have received new instructions. Apparently the Guardian is very impressed with your abilities and would like to meet you himself. How do you feel about a field trip?"

Alana jumped up, nearly knocking Hari off the bed with her breast.

"Ooof."

"Oh—sorry, Hari, but this is sooo exciting. Can I really meet the Guardian? Can I go with you two someplace, or will he come here? How's this going to work? Are you going to, like, scatter my particles and re-energize them or something? Like a transporter beam? Um—do I want that?" Thoughts burbled out of Alana's mouth so fast she lost track of them herself.

She only sputtered to a stop when she realized that once again, her genies were cracking themselves up with laughter.

"Hey—cut it out, you two." She smacked Hari gently upside the head and tugged Sami's ear. "I've never met a Guardian before—he's a pretty big honcho to you guys. I think it's thrilling..."

Trying hard to quell the giggles, Hari and Sami took deep breaths and resumed their positions as bookends to Alana's delightful library.

In an effort to concentrate, Sami focused on her breast this time, while Hari, sensualist that he was, cupped her mound and kept his hand still, allowing the warmth to penetrate to her still-recovering clit. It trembled slightly, recognizing the touch of a master.

"No, Alana, there is no transporting or anything—we are not aliens and this is not *Star Trek*. We will simply lie together and concentrate, and you will find your consciousness will travel elsewhere. There is a journey involved, but you will travel within our vessel, not an energizing beam. There is no Scotty. Our vessel does not, in fact, have any engines. Its purpose is not to travel through space so much as it is to navigate temporal distortions and..."

"Okay. Too much information, Hari. You lost me right after 'this is not *Star Trek*'. Just as long as I know it's safe. Oh—what do I wear? I do get clothes for this trip, right? I don't have to float through wormholes or whatever in my birthday suit...or some kind of early Turkish handkerchief..."

Sami closed his eyes and rested his head on her breast. Hari leaned his forehead on her shoulder.

"The essential woman. We should have known," he groaned.

"Well, it's important to me, guys. A girl has to look her best when meeting the Guardian, don't you think?"

Hari chuckled. "I don't think you need to worry on that score, Alana-delight. The Guardian has only permitted two other students to visit Anyela in our memory, so he must already think you are something quite special."

"He will love you as we do, Alana," added Sami with a quick lick to her sensitive skin. "But do not worry—we shall provide you with all you need."

"Perhaps it would be best for you to rest for a little while, this has been a physically challenging experience—especially for you, love..."

Hari slid his hand beneath her and caressed her naked buttocks. "Are you sore, Alana-sweet?"

Alana thought for a moment, examining her body's reactions. "Actually, no. Which I find quite surprising—I thought I wouldn't be able to sit down for a week."

"I promised you we'd not hurt you, didn't I?" said Sami. "Hari is very good at gauging how much you can take."

"Hari is very good, period. As are you, Sami. I have absolutely no complaints..." she smiled, and stifled a yawn.

"That is good to hear," smiled Sami.

He exchanged glances with Hari, who nodded. "Rest now, treasure of our hearts, you have a big day ahead of you..."

Sami leaned over and dropped the lightest of kisses on Alana's eyelids.

She slid bonelessly down from the pillows, sound asleep.

* * * * *

She awoke alone.

Tucked beneath the softest of comforters, Alana struggled back to consciousness and stretched her spine. Something was different. Perhaps it was the fact that she couldn't feel anything warm and hard and male next to her. She pouted and opened her eyes.

"Whoa, Toto—this definitely isn't Kansas..." she breathed, as she sat up and looked around.

No way was this the result of Sami's decorating magic.

She was in the middle of a very large bed, swathed with sheer hangings. The room seemed round on one side, with hundreds of little glass windows high up on the curved wall. The glass was in different colors, so the light glittering through caught the refracted tones and bounced them all over the place. It was a cross between a rainbow and a disco ball, and it made her pupils contract fiercely.

She rubbed her eyes and slid off the bed.

Beneath her feet was the most luxurious oriental carpet she'd ever seen. It almost seemed a sin to walk on it.

"You like my rug?"

Sami's voice startled her.

"It's exquisite, Sami. I've never seen anything quite so incredible…" She passed a toe delicately across a teal blue design. "The colors are so rich and bright."

"It's a favorite of mine. A gift, from someone special — long ago." There was something in his voice that caught Alana's attention, but before she could pursue it, Hari came in behind Sami with coffee in his hands.

"Greetings, Alana — and welcome to our home. Did you rest well? We decided on Sami's room for you, not for any special reason, but because he won the toss…"

Hari's smile could have charmed the shell off a turtle, and Alana couldn't help but smile back.

He crossed the room, took her in his arms and kissed her long and passionately.

"Wow," she breathed.

Sami pushed Hari out of the way. "My turn," he grinned, pressing his chest firmly against her naked breasts and devouring her mouth.

"Hmpf," squawked Alana, dropping onto the bed.

"God, you guys know how to wake a girl up in the morning, don't you?" Her breath returning, she looked at the coffee. "Is that for me? Or are we going to jump each other's bones here? I want to know, because I kind of like a schedule, and I want to see the rest of your home too…if that's okay? Not that I don't want sex, because I do, I mean, well right at this moment…um…"

Alana realized she was looking at them from the bottom of a rather large hole she'd just dug with her mouth.

"Where's the ladies room?"

Hari grinned, passed her the mug of coffee and led her to a door.

"Help yourself to whatever you need, Alana-love. When you're done go through that door," he gestured toward another opening, "and you'll find us."

Alana entered their bathroom with a great deal of curiosity.

It did seem, however, that Sami's exotic decorating touch didn't extend to creating an *Arabian Nights* themed bath.

The fixtures were lovely—a bath big enough for ten (at least), a large shower with a myriad of showerheads that shot water at just about every part of the body (gotta try that out), a toilet that looked just like—well, a toilet, and a massive vanity with many small cupboards around its huge central mirror. There were deep crimson towels folded neatly on a small vanity chair and a deep crimson rug on the floor.

The soaps, shampoos and lotions were all—no surprise—Blue Lotus. God, she had to take some of them back with her. She couldn't imagine being without that fragrance now.

The shower was as refreshing as she had guessed — she'd had to turn off a couple of the more personally-oriented jets — and she felt ready for anything as she toweled off the last drops of moisture and smoothed the Blue Lotus lotion all over her body.

She caught sight of herself in the mirror and paused.

She'd changed. Or had she? Her hair was the same, her face looked exactly as it had always looked. Her skin was glowing, but that could be the shower and the rub with the lovely bath towel.

She realized that she was holding her body differently. Her back was straighter, her breasts thrust forward with nipples taut and prominent, and her hips seemed curvier. She looked, in a word, sexual. She realized that what had changed was inside her, not outside. Her body was now sending out little pings of sexual sonar — she had a new awareness of what her body could do, and she liked it. Smiling, she sent up a prayer of thanks to the Patron Saint of Hallucinations. Whoever he was, he was certainly putting in overtime on this one.

It took moments for her to find Hari and Sami.

This must be their kitchen, she supposed, because there was an interesting blend of modern conveniences. There was a totally modern microwave — and a few antiques, including a cooking pot, which looked as if Caesar might have whipped up a stew in it, resting on a shelf.

The guys themselves lounged on stools that could have come from the most modern furniture store or Achmed's Bazaar a thousand years ago. Such was the nature of furniture. Form follows function. Alana grinned at the wayward thought.

"You are happy, love?" asked Hari as he moved toward her.

"I am clean, happy, feeling the caffeine do its job, and ready for anything," grinned Alana. "Do I get clothes yet?"

"Nope," answered Sami wickedly. "We don't dress indoors."

He was right. Both were splendidly naked, slightly aroused, and enough to make a girl cream her nonexistent knickers just from looking at them.

Alana sighed.

"Can I see the rest of your home before we get off track and into each other?" she asked wryly.

Sami chuckled and Hari grasped her hand.

"This way, Alana, let's satisfy your curiosity and then turn our attention to satisfying something else..." He smiled wickedly.

The vessel was surprisingly large.

The kitchen door led to a passage. Hari opened a door and said simply, "My room."

Alana peeked in. There was a definite touch of the austere, which suited Hari, she thought. Black and white ruled the day — a huge four-poster bed was draped in a black spread and covered with white cushions. Brass fixtures were scattered around the room and the windows at the top of Hari's wall were iridescent. The light that bounced in fractured into brilliance rather than color.

Alana's attention was caught by a painting — the only one on the wall — of a woman, sitting by a fountain, letting the water drip through her fingers. Light danced across her soft blonde hair and touched her beautiful breasts as she leaned over the ripples.

"Oh Hari, how lovely," she breathed, allowing her critical eye to absorb the mastery of the artist.

"Um…yeah. I like it," was all Hari said.

Alana registered his comment. Hmmm, she thought to herself. And again, hmmm.

Leaving Hari's room, they moved down the passage, passing what looked like an office or library, and into the large living area. There were comfortable, over-stuffed couches, a couple of well-used recliners, a large television and…yes…a cable box on top of it.

"We have only just learned of your DVD technology, and have secured a unit that will probably be installed when we arrive at Anyela," said Sami, waving at an unopened box, which loudly announced it contained Japanese technical equipment.

"Ah, testosterone rules," she muttered, smiling at the pride of the gender in high-tech.

She moved toward a beautiful display case—probably French, she mused, noting the elegant carvings and exquisite craftsmanship.

Proudly sitting by itself on one shelf was a glass flower.

She moved closer.

"This is truly amazing guys. What is it?"

Sami moved over to her side and opened the door to the cabinet.

"Is it Venetian? Murano maybe? Fifteenth century?" Her eyes were glued on the flower, spellbound by the light that trickled into the petals, bounced around the different shades of blue that drifted from a deep purplish-navy to a pale white blue, and then hit the vibrant yellow center.

It seemed almost alive as it rested on a swirl of flat green leaves.

"Your knowledge of such things is impressive, Alana," said Hari, moving to her side and pressing a kiss to her cheek.

"Yes, it is Venetian—early sixteenth century, actually, and commissioned for us by —by a friend. It is a Blue Lotus."

He said no more, and Alana glanced at him. He stared at the flower but she could tell his thoughts were elsewhere.

"I am glad you have gifts from your friends with you when you travel," she said gently, linking hands with both Hari and Sami and squeezing them.

"To judge by Sami's carpet and this flower, they care a great deal for you. Thank you for allowing me to see them."

Suddenly the room rocked a little and Alana gasped, glad that she had two strong hands to cling to.

Sami met Hari's gaze over Alana's head.

"We're here."

Chapter Sixteen

Alana stepped through a door into Paradise. Or at least what could well have passed for Paradise.

The first thing that struck her was the light. It was brilliant, very white, and reminded her of photos she'd seen of Greek islands, where the light seemed different than other places. She walked forward slowly, eyes wide, taking in her surroundings. It was nothing short of fantastic, in the real sense of the word.

There was color — color everywhere. Gardens spilled their blooms around her, massive trees offering shade, and smaller shrubs covered with incredibly tinted blooms. Gently guided by Hari and Sami, she moved down a stone path, feeling the warmth of the tiles caressing her bare feet.

She heard laughter ahead and the sound of water splashing. She turned and glanced at her companions, a question in her eyes.

"These are the Pleasure Gardens of Anyela," said Sami.

"This is where we spend some time in our youth and freedom, discovering the joys that giving and receiving pleasure can bring," added Hari, nodding down a path that led off to their left.

Alana followed his gaze. She saw a young couple in the dappled shade of some kind of giant palm tree, locked in an embrace that was incredibly passionate. It wasn't until the woman raised her leg to clasp the man's thigh that Alana realized he was buried deep inside as they kissed. Rocking back and forth, they moaned, completely oblivious to the world around them.

Hari encouraged Alana to move on.

"Let us allow them their pleasure, Alana-love. It is acceptable to explore the physical nature of love here, but not to treat it as a spectator sport — we try to maintain a little privacy — although…" Hari's eyebrow rose as they rounded a corner and passed an alcove containing a bench where an enthusiastic young man on his knees was devouring the pussy of a very receptive young woman.

"Perhaps things have become a little more open since we left, my brother," murmured Sami, walking Alana past the panting couple.

"What's *that*?" asked Alana, pointing at a magnificent structure that had just become visible in the distance. "It looks like the Taj Mahal's baby brother."

Sami grinned. "That is the Temple of Time, Alana-delight. The Guardian traditionally has his quarters there, and it is also the place where the wise men of our world gather to oversee the passing of time. None have seen it except for the Guardian and the Ancients who monitor such things."

They had reached a large open area — the smooth marble tiles underfoot had given way to soft terracotta — and fountains were splattering luminous water droplets everywhere. A large pool — more like a lake, really — was surrounded by urns overflowing with plants in every color she could imagine and some she couldn't. People were sitting, lying, reclining, and sprawling all over the place. There were some who were dressed, some partially so, and others completely nude. They shared one thing in common, thought Alana uncomfortably. They were all gorgeous.

She sucked in her stomach, only to let it out on a gasp as she watched one lovely woman cry out and writhe in the throes of orgasm at the hands of her lover. My goodness, thought Alana, I'm in the middle of a real-life orgy. No, she amended, watching a nubile young woman with delicately green-shaded skin and blue hair shed her silks and scamper into the water, followed by an amazingly erect young man with beautifully sculpted buns. Make that Club-Med, galactic- style.

More trees, some palms, some looking like weeping willows with huge white flowers hanging from their branches, clustered along the boundaries of the water, offering shade to those who had chosen to lie on the many floating leaves. And what leaves they were. Some were over six feet across, and about as far from a frog's lily pad as Alana could ever have guessed. These leaves were occupied by all kinds of people in just about every position of sexual ecstasy.

There were couples enjoying the simple pleasures of straightforward fucking, sending ripples across the water to others who enjoyed the rocking motion as they, in turn, found their pleasure.

Other pads held a single occupant, trailing legs in the water, while a partner's head nestled between their thighs.

"How deep is that water?" asked Alana, the thought of drowning while coming crossing her ever-practical mind as she watched two lovely silver beings frolic all over each other above the water and then sink with a moan beneath the surface.

"Not very, and they are all taught to swim as children, Alana," said Sami.

"Children? You have children here?" Alana turned, shocked, to Hari and Sami.

"Of course we have children here, Alana."

"Not *here*, as in here…" added Hari, waving his hands at the scene of lustful sensuality before them. "This is strictly for unmated adults—a place where we can explore sex, and love, and learn about such things without restraint."

"But the rest of Anyela is a settled, productive world," said Sami.

"If you look over there," he pointed to the distance, "you'll see the hillsides of the vineyards, and further on, over on the other side of those hills, are the fertile plains where we have farms. There are high mountains for enjoyment and the occasional hunt — although we do not, as a rule, eat meat here—only when the herds get out of hand…"

"So marriage and family are permitted here?"

"Of course," said Sami.

"Indeed they are," added Hari.

"In fact, the Sages of our land must have families, and have established themselves as productive members of Anyelan society before they are allowed to become Ancients and join the Monitors of Time."

Alana turned her attention back to the crowd that was frolicking around her. The women wore colorful versions of her own clothing that Sami and Hari had created for her before they left the vessel. At least, the ones who were wearing clothes did.

A scrap of silk sat low on the hips, and a matching vest was loosely tied between the breasts—nothing that could interfere with access to the important pleasure points of a woman's body, thought Alana, her own growing warm at the idea.

The men were even more simply clad—a straight skirt wrapped around lean hips and across a flat torso, falling to mid thigh. Cool, comfortable and vaguely Roman in appearance, it also seemed ready to fall off when necessary, and certainly allowed the excitement of the wearer to show through—several that Alana could see were tented in a very impressive fashion, as their owners became increasingly aroused.

"Hmmm. This place has potential," she murmured, more to herself than anyone else.

"Excuse me, Alana-love..." Hari grabbed her firmly by the elbow and led her away from the scene of naked decadence and toward a side grotto. His hands slipped under her vest and caressed her breast.

"Remember who brought you, sweet delight." He nipped her neck playfully.

Sami brought her face around and kissed her long and hard. "Don't forget *us*, Alana," he whispered huskily.

"As if I could," she breathed, holding them both tight to her body for a second and enjoying the warmth of their flesh against hers.

Hari stopped them in front of a large gong. "It is time," he said. "We must let the Guardian know we have returned with our special guest."

Holding Alana's hand, and putting his other hand firmly on her buttocks, Sami moved her to one side as Hari reached for the mallet hanging down beside the gong.

He struck a resounding blow and Alana winced slightly as the ringing tone billowed around them.

He moved to stand on Alana's other side, drawing her arm through his in a strangely formal way.

The ringing of the gong had brought a new level to the noise of chatter and laughter, and within moments, Alana, Sami and Hari were surrounded by smiling faces calling welcome and greetings to all of them. The tension she had felt from her guys drained away, and Hari and Sami were soon surrounded by their people. Alana noticed the look of awe on many a face as they bid welcome to the travelers — obviously Hari and Sami had spoken the truth when they announced that they were the best at what they do.

The chatter increased in volume, accompanied by much laughter and good-natured teasing. Alana stood back, glad to be able to have a moment to watch this homecoming for the two men she had grown to love so much.

She noticed two women hanging back from the crowd, yet both with eyes fixed on the tall genies as they laughed and kissed and clapped hands on bare shoulders.

One, a petite beauty, with blue eyes and sun streaked ash-brown hair, said something to the other, only to be met with a fierce shake of the head. Touching her shoulder, the blue-eyed lovely moved forward with purpose. Alana gasped as she recognized her blonde companion — it was the woman from Hari's painting.

"Greetings, Honored Sami, we give thanks at your safe return," said a quiet voice, as the vivid eyes of this beautiful woman gazed at Sami.

Paling, Sami held out his hand. "It is good to see you here, Debalhi, you are still... still unmated then?"

"I have found no one to bring me pleasure, Sami, not for many turns of the moons now..." Neither she nor Sami seemed to realize that they were still firmly clasping hands.

"My father has several new and fine rugs, you might wish to visit his shop before you leave again—perhaps there might be something you would like..." Her voice petered out as Sami's blue gaze devoured her, passing over her breasts like a hot flame and making her nipples stand out through the pale yellow silk of her vest.

Alana quirked a mental eyebrow, surprised to see such naked emotion on Sami's face—he who had merrily sucked her clit and shouted out his climax to the world was clinging onto one woman's hand like it was his life preserver.

Hmmmm.

Emboldened by her friend's success, the other woman drew a breath and approached Hari.

"Welcome home, Hari," she said.

Hari's face betrayed none of his feelings, but his eyes—oh yes, thought Alana, that's where they show. Burning with unvoiced passion, Hari stared long and hard at the woman before him.

"It is good to be home, Pemalina," he said, voice husky. Then he placed his hands on her shoulders and drew her close, just brushing her lips with his.

Alana saw her fists clench as if fighting the urge to grab him and hold him tight to those lovely breasts that trembled at his closeness.

Both Hari and Sami couldn't hide their erections—out of the crowds of beautiful and naked people, only two women had elicited this kind of response. Alana knew she was looking at the "friends" whose gifts traveled with Hari and Sami throughout their journeys.

Hmmmm again, she thought, mind working furiously.

Hari and Sami wrenched themselves back into the moment as the crowd surged around Alana, smiling, welcoming, patting, kissing, touching—she would have felt swamped and nervous if it hadn't been for the fact that there was such incredible happiness shining from all these lovely faces.

"Um…nice to meet you all," she muttered, trying not to notice the large number of bare breasts and jutting cocks that bobbed about quite cheerfully.

She felt her genies come to her side protectively, and breathed a little sigh of relief as the crowd moved back.

However, it was not to give her room that the people were moving—it was to make way for a new arrival.

He strode boldly down the path toward Alana, the sun glinting on his tumble of shoulder length black hair and sparking off the silver that glinted at his temples. He wore black silk loose pants, slung very low on his hips, and an open silk tunic which fell from his broad shoulders, catching the breeze as he walked and billowing out on either side. His chest was a thing of beauty with the lightest touch of black hair scattered over solid flesh, narrowing to a thin line pointing down to his trousers. He was barefoot, gorgeous, and Alana's entire body tightened with arousal as he neared her.

"You!" she gasped as she recognized him. "You sold me the vessel."

"Alana, may we present—the Guardian," said Sami, bowing low.

The others followed suit, bowing low before this man who held so much power in his hands. Gone were the elegant business suit and the charming demeanor of a gallery owner. Now there was nothing but raw sexuality, and an intelligent energy that surrounded him like heat.

His eyes were nearly black and burned into Alana from beneath straight brows. Gazing at him squarely in the face, Alana noticed the touch of arrogance in the angle of his chin, and the way his moustache and goatee tilted at her in an almost accusing fashion.

"Greetings, Miss West," he said, in a rather disinterested tone. "Welcome to Anyela."

Alana found herself on the horns of a dilemma. Long a vocal opponent of what she liked to call "arrogant managerial machismo," she found herself face-to-face with someone who really looked like he was a prime candidate for the title. On the other hand, her body was encouraging her to rip off her clothes, lie down, spread her legs and beg him to fuck her brains out. What to do?

"It's a pleasure to be here, Mr. Guardian..." she began, not sure how one addressed the "Guardian" of a time portal. *That* never got covered in *Cosmo's* Q and A columns.

"I'm sure it is," he drawled. "Now let's get to the ceremony, shall we?" He turned away abruptly and strode off down another path.

"Well," snorted Alana, hands on hips. "I hope he's better at guarding time than he is on manners."

Hari and Sami winced.

"Alana, he carries many grave burdens and is as close to a ruler as we have here. It is his right to be that way if he chooses."

"Hmpf... Not if he wants loyal and happy subjects. How does he know people won't get upset if he acts like that and try and stage a coup or something?"

She was interrupted by a chokingly orgasmic cry as they passed a couple seated on top of each other.

"Well okay, people might be a bit too busy for a revolution, but there's still no excuse for that kind of...of...*attitude*..." She flounced off the path after the Guardian, leaving Hari and Sami to follow. She was quite aware that two silent women had also decided to join the group, but said nothing as they walked on.

They reached what seemed to be a public square of some kind—open buildings housed storefronts offering many different selections of merchandise—it was a shopper's heaven and Alana's fingers itched to browse.

"Later, Alana—attend to the Guardian's words, please," urged Hari, directing her attention away from the stalls.

"Urgh," she groaned. "This is truly torture."

The Guardian had stepped onto a low dais and was waiting for the crowd to assemble.

"Candidates for the role of Qualifier, stand forward," barked the Guardian.

A sizeable number of very nicely hung young men dropped their silks and stepped forward. Goodness, thought Alana. This could get interesting.

Hari and Sami stepped away from Alana's side — she felt their movement rather than saw it, and turned with a sound of distress.

"It is now time for you to undergo the graduation ceremony, Alana. We can do no more but tell you that you are in our hearts…" The looks on their faces were almost identical — a blend of pride, passion and sadness.

This was the end of her journey with them, she realized, and her eyes filled with tears.

"Alana West," said the Guardian loudly. "You have been selected to fulfill the Graduation Ceremony here on Anyela. At the conclusion of this ceremony you will be granted permanent possession of all the abilities you have learned over the past period of time in company with our two delegates, Hari and Sami." He nodded in their direction, and they bowed their heads respectfully.

"Your life will change for the better — you will be filled with the knowledge of the pleasure you can give and receive and you will play an important role in the future of your timeline, although we cannot divulge to you what that role will be."

His black-eyed gaze rested on Alana, sending sensual shivers down her abdomen to her clit. She knew her body was moistening and was helpless to stop it. This damn Guardian could probably make her come just by looking at her.

"Understanding all these benefits, are you now ready to begin the Graduation Ceremony?"

Alana took a deep breath as an idea crystallized into a plan deep within her.

Gazing right back into the Guardian's eyes, she raised her head.

"No."

Chapter Seventeen

The silence that fell was total. Not a leaf rustled in the luxuriant vegetation that surrounded the square, nor a body twitched amongst the people who had been shocked into immobility.

The Guardian stared at Alana, and for one second she felt a—presence—of sorts within her mind. His eyes narrowed.

"You have refused this gift we offer you?"

"Yes, I…"

"You are within your rights to do so." The Guardian looked at the crowd that was beginning to murmur in disbelief.

"This woman has the right to refuse—just as we have the right to suggest that she reconsider this decision."

"But, I want…"

The Guardian ignored her.

"Take her to the Loom."

He strode off the dais without a backward glance, as two rather confused men came to either side of Alana and grasped her arms firmly.

"But I didn't get to…"

"You must come with us, Mistress Alana," they said respectfully, quite failing to meet her eyes.

She glanced around, only to see Hari and Sami with expressions of worry creasing their handsome faces. The crowd was holding them back from her.

She glanced around at the throng. They were beautiful, loving, free beings—her eyes passed over Debalhi and Pemalina, who were also looking very concerned. She knew she was doing the right thing.

Raising her head, she nodded at her two guards and allowed them to lead her out of the square toward a small grotto. Head up, back straight, she gave her best impression of Marie Antoinette on the way to the guillotine. Okay—bad analogy here. She stumbled slightly. This couldn't possibly be a world that endorsed capital punishment—could it?

She breathed a sigh of relief as they reached what was obviously "the Loom." It was being hastily cleaned of its yarns prior to her arrival, and was, indeed, a loom of sorts. The main structure was a free-standing square of about six feet—the threads were wrapped around the top bar and a moveable one on the bottom—the shuttle would be passed between as the bar moved—she assumed. She did remember something of that tour she'd taken of early weaving machines. And who said museums never taught anything useful.

Now, however, the Loom was destined for a different purpose. Alana was led to the dais upon which it stood, and placed directly beneath it. Her arms were raised and attached to the top bar by soft ropes, and her feet were pulled apart and attached to a spreader bar—again the cuffs for her ankles were soft and silky. She was not in any pain, but knew the position would probably become uncomfortable if she had to stay there for any length of time.

The last touch was a black silk blindfold.

Deprived of her sight, she felt more vulnerable and a lot more nervous now than she had just moments before.

"Alana West," came the magisterial tones of the Guardian.

"You have refused the privilege of accepting our bounty. We now offer you the chance to change your mind. Should you continue to refuse, punishment will be inflicted — we will not despoil your body, but we will encourage you to see the error of your ways. I ask you now, before the assembled citizens of Anyela, will you accept our terms?"

Alana straightened her spine and turned in the direction of the Guardian's voice.

"I do not accept these terms. I want to..."

"She refuses," interrupted the Guardian. "The punishment will begin."

Murmurs rumbled through the crowd as Alana felt her clothes being gently removed.

"You will be the object of discipline for our subjects. They are now free to exercise their skills with an assortment of different tools on your body — they are not to penetrate you or bring you to orgasm at any time. To do so is to take your place on the Loom."

Alana heard his footsteps slapping away from her as her mind tried to absorb what he had said.

Tools — she wondered — oh, God, what tools?

She was just about to find out.

"Mistress, this will be difficult for many of us," came a quiet voice at her side.

She heard the soft sounds of movement and then felt a stinging lash across her buttocks. It was some kind of whip.

But there were little knots on the end, and if administered correctly, these knots whipped around her hips and just stung her clit enough to arouse it. Oh *gawd*...

"Mistress, please understand that we do not do this to hurt you," said another voice.

She braced herself.

This time it was a paddle, a sharp slap to her bottom that made her cheeks burn.

Within the space of an hour, she was trembling, her clit aroused to the point of pain and her buttocks on fire.

When several minutes had passed with no more takers for the whips and paddles routine, she allowed herself to slump a little, and dropped her head forward.

"Mistress Alana, may we help you for a few moments? It is allowed — if you would care to use our facilities..."

A tentative touch on her arm roused Alana.

"That would be most welcome," she said, determined to be as gracious as a naked woman with a red backside could be.

Gentle hands freed her wrists and ankles and helped her off the dais, untying the blindfold as they did.

The light startled her for a moment and she blinked rapidly. There, at either side, were the two women who had captured the hearts of Alana's genies. They were helping her straighten her cramped muscles as she stretched and groaned.

"Are you all right?" asked Debalhi, her blue eyes worriedly looking over Alana's body.

"I'll live," sighed Alana. "How long does this go on?"

"We do not know, Mistress," said Pemalina, glancing up through her blonde lashes as she finished untying the ankle cuffs. "No one has ever been punished on the Loom before — at least not that we remember." She helped Alana walk slowly along a narrow path to a small white building.

It was cool and shady inside, and Alana saw with pleasure that it was both a bathroom and a shower facility. She heaved a sigh of relief as she whisked herself into the private cubicle, only to wince as her sore buttocks touched the cool surface of the seat.

"Ow!" she hissed.

"We have a soothing lotion here, Alana — it may help. Occasionally we get too much sun and it makes that pain go away. I'm sure it will help soothe your — er — skin," called Debalhi

Alana left the cubicle and moved toward a large counter where water splashed from an ornately carved fish. To her surprise the water was warm and fragrant — she rubbed her hands under it with pleasure.

"Would you like to refresh yourself with a shower, Alana?" Debalhi nodded toward the rear of the room where a beautifully tiled area was set aside for the fountain of sparkling and glittering water that was jetting out from high on the wall.

"Would I ever! You guys are lifesavers."

Alana walked right into the stream of water. One of the advantages of being naked — no time wasted on undressing. She stood and relished the warm droplets that bounced from her shoulders and nose, and used the soap (Blue Lotus, of course) that was set in a recessed dish nearby.

Feeling quite human again, except for a rather sore bum, she walked out, toweling herself with one of the soft cloths Pemalina had offered her.

"Lie here, Alana—let us put some lotion on your poor cheeks…" Debalhi's worried voice touched Alana's heart and she lay, face down, on her towel that she'd draped over a stone bench.

The touch of their hands and the feel of the lotion were heaven.

"So tell me, guys, how long have you two been in love with Hari and Sami?"

The hands that had been delicately stroking her buttocks froze.

"Alana…I…we…I mean, what do you…?"

"Oh Jeez, I'm sorry. I didn't mean to embarrass you." Alana looked over her shoulder at two pained faces.

"It's as clear as a bell that you're crazy about them, and they're just as nuts about you."

"You truly think so?"

"Bet my last buck on it…" said Alana definitively.

"What's a buck?"

"Never mind. Just tell me how you came to fall in love with those two sweethearts?"

Pemalina snorted inelegantly, rather at odds with her hazel-eyed, fragile beauty. "You've seen them, and you've had sex with them. Where's the question?"

"Well yeah, sure, they're gorgeous, great in bed, etcetera. But you really *love* them, don't you?"

"Don't you?" asked Debalhi, resuming her application of the lotion, and not too gently this time.

"Of course I do. I couldn't help it—I was their assignment. But I knew it was just that—a temporary assignment. If I could save the memories of being with them forever I would—they are a part of my heart now and I should hate to lose that. But you guys must have met and fallen in love differently— it's not the same for you, living here in Anyela, is it? Why haven't you married, or mated, or swapped lotus-oaths or whatever it is you do here..."

Pemalina sighed.

"I met Hari when he rescued me from slave traders on the Arabic peninsula. He had just finished one of his early assignments when his journey took him across the path of the caravan I was in. My master, the man who had purchased me, was displeased and was taking it out on me. Had Hari not saved me, I'd surely be dead."

Pemalina paused in her story to close her eyes tight against the tears that threatened to fall.

"How could I not love him? I owe him my life, and on our journey home he showed me that I was still a woman, a desirable woman, and in doing so he captured my heart for all time. I am honored that he loves me in return, but his duty is to Anyela and the genie program—he is not free to mate."

Alana looked at Debalhi. "You too?"

Debalhi nodded. "Sami helped me escape from a funeral pyre near my home in India. I had been wed the day before to an elderly man from a neighboring village. I was barely seventeen. When he died, I was to join him—it was considered an honor to die with one's husband.

Needless to say, I didn't consider 'Suthi' to be much of an honor, and I was only too happy to see Sami as he leapt through the flames and whisked me off the top of the pyre. To this day, I don't know whether my disappearance was ever noticed. But Sami noticed me. We have spent many happy hours together—he loves the rugs my father makes in his little store. And I am happy to think that he loves me a little too…"

She modestly dropped her eyes and a blush spread over her fine breasts.

"Your father? Wouldn't he be in India?"

"This is Anyela, Mistress. We have different customs here. When someone is brought here, there are many choices available to them. I chose to become part of a family—I love to work with yarns and rugs, and I was welcomed. Pem, here, loves children—she became a teacher in one of our schools."

Alana sighed.

"Okay—I'm going to ask something of you two—I'd like you to trust me. Will you believe me when I tell you I think I'm going to be able to solve your problems?"

She raised herself gingerly onto the towel, pleasantly surprised when her backside didn't scream at her.

"What do you mean, Alana?" asked Debalhi.

"I can't tell you exactly what I'm going to do, because I don't have all the details worked out, but I have a pretty good notion…."

Her eyes narrowed as she looked at the two girls sitting in front of her.

"Tell me what the graduation process entails?"

"Well," began Pemalina, crossing her legs comfortably. "We have a special tree— the Tree of Ecstasy. At its base is a tangled shelf of branches that has grown to form a bed. This tree is always in bud, but never blooms unless a couple attains a very high level of sexual satisfaction in the bed beneath. I can't remember the last time it flowered, can you?" She raised an eyebrow at Debalhi.

"Nope."

"So you, as a graduate of our program, will lie on this bed with one of the Qualifiers of your choosing and see if you can make the tree bloom. That's all there is to it."

"Aha. And who are these Qualifiers?"

"They are males who are unmatched, and who have distinguished themselves in a variety of areas— lovemaking, oral sex, sports, academics, things like that."

"Okay—let me see if I have this straight. I get to pick an Anyelan hot stud, go for a roll in the hay—excuse me— branches of this tree, and if the earth shakes, fireworks explode and the tree blooms, I graduate?"

Debalhi raised an eyebrow. "Well, I think you've got the basics. I'm not sure about the earth and the fireworks thing, though, and the tree probably won't bloom— usually it's just a couple of extra petals showing."

"Punishment is to recommence," boomed a loud voice.

"Damn—I'm really starting to get pissed off at that guy," muttered Alana, recognizing the strident tones of the Guardian.

"Thanks, girls. I appreciate what you've done—and I want you to know that I don't think there are two better, nicer, or sweeter guys around than Hari and Sami. You'd better make them happy or you'll have me to reckon with."

Alana put her arms around the shoulders of the two women and gave them each a quick hug. It was hard to know that these were the women who had captured the hearts of her favorite genies, but then again, all good hallucinations must come to an end sometime.

On that cheerful thought, Alana strode nakedly back to the loom and waggled her ass at the crowd just for kicks.

Chapter Eighteen

Within two hours, Alana's butt was burning again, and her clit was so aroused that her juices were trickling down her legs. Her waggling instincts had long gone. The weapon of choice for the afternoon had been the whip, and some of its wielders had been very skilled and a little over-enthusiastic, flicking her swollen tissue accurately and stimulatingly time after time.

She felt the breeze cooling her shoulders and guessed that the sun was beginning to go down—or was it suns? She couldn't remember how many there were.

Suddenly a hard chest was behind her and a very solid and familiar cock was thrusting between her cheeks.

"Alana-love, why are you doing this?" Hari nipped her earlobe gently as he rubbed slowly up and down along her cleft, being careful not to further abrade her skin.

"Omar's balls, why don't you just say yes to the Guardian, delight?" murmured Sami in a worried voice, coming up in front of her and sandwiching her between them.

His cock tented his trousers and Alana moaned as he rubbed against her.

"We should not be doing this, but we cannot allow you to suffer…" muttered Sami as he pressed his cock against her wet flesh.

Hari's hands slipped around and fondled her breasts as Sami continued his pressure on her pussy.

Alana moaned.

"Oh God, guys...you feel so good..."

"You are not supposed to orgasm, dear one, but we cannot permit you to go unfulfilled—you are still our student—we must help you if we can." And Hari opened his trousers so that the warm velvet of his cock could caress her cleft freely.

Sami also flipped the fastening on his silks, and slid himself over Alana's wet and sensitive clit.

They moaned in unison as an orgasm rocked the three of them simultaneously. To her amazement, she found herself the recipient of two helpings of creamy cum.

"Wow. No fog," she whispered, as Hari gently wiped her clean and removed her blindfold.

She raised her eyes and looked at both of them.

"This is Anyela, Alana. Here, we can function as ordinary men—we can create life."

Had she any doubts as to her current plan, they would have completely disappeared at that moment. She knew that her course was absolutely right.

"My God, this place is something else. The chocolate must be divine," she mumbled, considering the many benefits of living in such a paradise.

"Chocolate?" asked Sami.

"We don't have chocolate in Anyela, love," added Hari.

Alana gaped at them. "No chocolate?"

Sami shook his head.

"No Godiva? No Dove bars? No Hershey kisses? "

"Uh-uh," answered Sami.

"Didn't you ever bring any back with you?"

"Well, we tried once or twice, but it never made it back. We, er, ate it on the way."

"Oh really?"

"Well, how do you share chocolate with thousands of people?" asked Sami, with a rather embarrassed cough.

"And the plants don't grow here for some reason," added Hari.

Alana was quiet for a moment.

"You guys have given me an idea," she whispered. "But you'd better go before you get in trouble. Just tell me this…" she stopped them with a gaze.

"Do you two love Debalhi and Pemalina?"

Incredibly, both beautiful, hunky, bodies-to-die-for, magically powered genies blushed.

"They are very special to us, Alana," said Hari quietly, his deep brown eyes glowing.

"We have a — a — there is something strong between us," admitted Sami.

"Then — trust me," said Alana. "You have given me so much — let me return the favor." She jumped as she heard voices nearing the grotto.

"I love you guys — I always will. Please be careful."

They kissed her soundly, re-tied her blindfold and then left. Alana turned her head away as her eyes filled with tears, knowing that she had to let them go, but hating the thought of never being with them again.

Then the voices materialized into two brawny young men who were excited at the thought of trying out a couple of new toys, and for the next hour or so, Alana felt the gentle sting of the whip again.

* * * * *

It was not hard to sense that the sun had set when Alana finally found herself alone. The air had cooled considerably—for which her ass was sincerely thankful. The light no longer penetrated her blindfold, and the light rustle of the daylight creatures had given way to the low hum of the night.

Alana's senses were on full alert as she caught the slight sound of a skimming foot on tiles.

"I should have known I was going to have a problem with you," came a soft and rather regretful voice.

Her head jerked up at his words.

"Guardian?"

"Yes," he answered, standing close behind her and just brushing his fingers up her spine.

She shivered and her nipples puckered.

"I want to share something with you, Alana," he murmured, sliding his hands around her waist and raising them until her breasts rested comfortably on his palms.

"What, no whips or chains?" she snorted.

He smothered a chuckle in her neck. God, he smelled wonderful.

"No, not this time—just wait for a moment..." One hand released a breast and moved upwards to untie her blindfold. She blinked, trying to get her eyes to function in the darkness.

Soon she could make out the silhouettes of the trees against the night sky, and the beginnings of a moonrise— or several moonrises—God, this was strange. The stars were beautiful but different, and the sound of the nighttime insects had risen to a whiny drone.

"Wait for it, Alana," he breathed into her ear, sending shudders down her vertebrae.

He delicately fondled her nipples, bringing them to their sensitive and swollen peak. His body pressed closer to her back, warming her.

He was aroused, no two ways about it. A huge cock was pressing against her cleft, but he was certainly aware of her discomfort and taking steps to ensure he didn't hurt her. Alana's clit throbbed—God, she'd like to get some of that cock where it would do the most good.

The Guardian's hand slid down past her navel to her pussy and a strong and certain finger began to play.

She gasped, unable to do more than writhe her hips a little.

"Sssh…relax—wait for the Tal Shayla."

"What's that, another word for camel orgasm?" she hissed, trying to get his hand to move just a *fraction* to the left.

"Oh no. Wait now—any second…"

Any second and she was going to explode, she thought. He slipped a finger into her soaking pussy and massaged the tender walls. A second finger joined in the fun and unerringly sought out her special spot—she squirmed as he finger-fucked her into insanity.

Suddenly a loud whirring sound began.

Alana gasped as thousands upon thousands of fireflies all lit up their little insect butts at once and flew up into the still night air. Instead of the warm yellow gold flashes of Earth, these were striking silver blue—their light filled the night sky. With a whirring shriek there seemed to be a mighty explosion and a glittering rain fell over the trees, the lake, Alana and the Guardian.

Alana's body gave way and she leaned into an orgasm that kept her on her toes for long shuddering minutes.

The Guardian held her close, waiting for her to ride out the aftermath of her climax.

"Wow," she breathed, leaning back on him.

"Wow indeed, my sweet," he answered, untying her from her restraints.

She staggered, only to find herself caught up in strong arms and carried a short distance to a convenient and secluded chaise.

"What was that all about?" she asked, as the Guardian settled her in his lap and pulled a soft silk blanket around her shoulders.

"Those are Shayla bugs, Alana. They fly into the heart of the night—they light the way for their females. Then they mate. The resulting shower is said to enhance an orgasm. I believe you would agree?"

Alana was silent for a moment, digesting this.

"Wait, you mean I'm covered with bug cum?" she asked, struggling to sit up.

A rich laugh broke the night, and he hugged her to his chest.

"No, no. The flies release their lighted sections when they mate—it's some kind of chemical thing—completely harmless, and no, you're not covered in bug cum." He chuckled again. "You're covered with my favorite blanket, and resting with me on my favorite chair. Were it not dark, you would be able to see my home and much of Anyela from this spot — I come here when I wish to think."

His hand slid under the blanket and found her warm buttocks. He absently stroked them soothingly, and Alana found that the throbbing was easing. She turned slightly to give him better access.

"Oooh…that feels so good," she muttered, burying her nose into his neck.

The Guardian sighed.

"I applaud your courage, Alana. It's a good plan."

She stilled in his arms.

"How did you know?"

He chuckled again, a rich rumble against her body, and pulled her even tighter to his chest. "I am the Guardian. I know everything."

"Oh, yeah?" Her feminist instincts went to red-alert status.

"Yeah, honey," he soothed.

"Well…jeez…Mr. Modesty, what are you—a mind reader of some kind?" she blustered, having remembered that she was, in fact, cuddling naked on the lap of the Guardian of Time, not some jerk who'd just announced he was invincible at Trivial Pursuit.

"In some ways, yes. I sensed your feelings when you denied our honor this morning—you were doing it for the very best of reasons, weren't you?"

Alana rested her head back against his shoulder with a defeated sigh.

"I just wanted to make a deal," she whispered.

"I know, sweet delight, I know," he crooned, cuddling her and stroking her. "Your thoughts gave you away—the love and gratitude I felt inside you would have made me grant it right away if I could have," he answered.

"Then why didn't you? Why all the fuss with the Loom and the whips, and my poor aching ass?"

"Still aching, Alana?" he asked as his fingers danced magically down her cleft, caressing dark and intimate places with an amazing skill.

She squirmed, amazed to find herself aroused again and with no pain at all in her buttocks.

"Mmm, I guess not," she murmured with a smile.

"I could not allow you to challenge me at that moment, Alana. Please try to understand. What you will ask of me has never been asked before. I had to demonstrate that you were willing to stand up and fight for what you wanted, and that I was strong enough to sentence you to be punished for defying me."

Alana thought about that.

"Do you have some kind of God complex? People say no to you and you have them decapitated?"

His body shook with laughter.

"How I wish I could keep you here, Alana—you are a delight to all my senses…"

He broke into another laugh.

"I'm serious—you may have some issues here. If your people can't say no to you, you need to revamp your managerial style, buddy, I'm telling you…" said Alana, getting into her "don't-mess-with-me-I'm-a-new-millennium-woman" mode.

"Alana-delight, my people are quite free to disagree with me on any number of issues, and they most usually do. I do not 'rule' here, I am merely the Guardian of Time. By virtue of my job, I have become sort of a President of Anyela, if you will, but I cannot order decapitations—" he stifled another laugh, "—even though sometimes I wish I could."

Alana wriggled slightly, enjoying the feel of his very nice cock beneath her thighs. He was partially aroused, she could tell, and yet he was stroking her body in a soothing and non-sexual fashion. It was rather nice, she decided, relaxing even more.

"So tomorrow, when I come to you again, you may ask for your boon to be granted —I shall be pleased to listen, and then the ceremony will commence. Is that fair enough?"

"I still don't see why I had to wait," she groused, but rather calmly. His voice and his hands were working magic on her.

"Because your boon will affect how we manage the Time disruptions, Alana. This is not a matter to be taken lightly. Had you not come here with the goal of freeing Hari and Sami from their duty to Anyela, I don't know how I would have been able to accomplish it."

Chapter Nineteen

"You knew. You really did read my mind."

Alana's breath seemed to have left her body. The shock at hearing her plan, so carefully nurtured, casually drop from the lips of the Guardian, had knocked her for the proverbial loop.

"It was quite apparent from the feelings I sensed between you and your genies that there was a special bond. What other reason could you possibly have for refusing our offerings?"

Alana placed her hand on his firm chest and absently ran her fingers through the soft whorls of hair.

"So you wanted to release them too," she said.

"Indeed I did. They are the best genies that Anyela has yet seen—I knew there would be severe opposition amongst the ancients who rely on their talents to straighten out the kinks in the space-time continuum—"

"Or add a few," interrupted Alana with a little giggle.

The Guardian dropped a laughing kiss on top of her head.

"Or add a few. They are a very inventive team, those two."

"You have no idea," said Alana with feeling.

"But the Ancients have forgotten what it is to love—to mate—to see one's woman grow large with one's child—to start a dynasty that may well produce a new Guardian of

Time…" He stopped for a moment and gazed into the darkness.

"Guardian?" Alana raised a tentative hand to his face and brushed the prickly softness of his goatee.

"Hmmm?"

"What about you? Do you have a family? Children? A wife?"

"Once upon a time, my sweet, once upon a time."

"But not here in Anyela?" she pressed, shrewdly judging his tone of voice.

"No, Alana, not here in Anyela. Here the rules are different, and the Guardian of Time is different again. But enough of this."

He pulled her close and brought her hand to his lips. His tongue swirled around in her palm and she gasped at the bolt of lightning that zapped her loins.

"Oh my," she breathed, unable to take her eyes off him in spite of the deepening gloom around them.

"It's been a long day for you, treasured Alana. And I think tomorrow may well be even longer. You need to rest if you are to make the Ecstasy flowers bloom."

"But I want to know…"

She got no further, as the Guardian bent and gently touched her lips with his. He tasted of honey and cinnamon and man and some other wonderful things she couldn't put a name to. She just knew she wanted more.

Opening her lips she welcomed his tongue as it slid into her mouth, learning, flicking, tantalizing, seducing— she was shaking with arousal within moments. He eased away from her and dropped little soothing kisses on her eyelids.

"You are a special person, Alana. It is good that you are here in Anyela. Sleep now."

Her head dropped on his shoulder, her eyes closed, and she slept.

* * * * *

Trumpets were blaring in her ears. Okay, this was it—Pearly Gates, St. Peter, hosts of angels—she really was dead.

On the other hand, if she were dead, she probably wouldn't have such a pressing need to pee.

Alana groggily rose up on one elbow to see two women looking nervously at her. "Would you care to accompany us to the bathing chamber, Mistress Alana? We have been instructed to see to your needs…"

Had she been able to, she would have leapt off the chaise and kissed them both soundly. However, her legs were still a bit stiff, her shoulders ached slightly, and she was unsure about the state of her butt cheeks.

So it was a very cautious Alana who rose grandly from her chaise, glancing around for the Guardian. He was gone. She had been tucked up in his blankets and slept the night away. She sighed.

A shower and some judicious lotion application took care of the worst of her aches and pains—surprisingly her backside was almost healed. She'd expected welts and perhaps a little bruising, but thanks to the Guardian's gentling touch, she felt as good as new. She enjoyed a light breakfast that had been placed just outside for her. The women helped her into a formal robe—of vivid yellow silk, it fell to her feet and tied at the waist with an elegant golden cord. Some bathrobe, she thought, as she finished her coffee. Bloomingdale's would kill for this line.

She left the bathing chamber on their heels, following them back to what she recognized as the town square.

A crowd had gathered, and more were coming. Everybody wanted to get a look at the notorious woman who had defied the Guardian.

She straightened her spine and looked ahead, seeing the Guardian waiting for her in his usual black silk.

She neared the dais and raised her eyes to his. He seemed very formal this morning—there was little sign of the man who had aroused her and caressed her so gently last night.

The crowd quieted as the Guardian raised his hand.

"Mistress Alana. You are welcome again before the people of Anyela. Yesterday you were offered the gifts that are ours to bestow, yet you refused. Would you care to reconsider your opinion?"

His voice echoed around the shops and the flowers, the crowd was silent, waiting for Alana's reply.

Alana stepped to the dais and looked at him. Something twinkled in the back of his eyes and gave her the courage she needed.

"Guardian," she began, rather nervously. "I have indeed had time to meditate on your offer, and have enjoyed the attentions of the good people of Anyela..." She waved her hand at the crowd, some of whom blushed, a couple of whom dropped their heads.

Got you, you little buggers, she thought. I remember you—you were the ones who got a bit whip-happy yesterday.

The Guardian glanced at them sharply.

Damn, he *can* read minds.

"If I may be permitted to address these good people and yourself?" she continued, a rather evil grin lurking somewhere on behalf of her butt. Payback would be sweet.

"You are granted permission," said the Guardian.

"I would like to say how honored I am to be here in your beautiful Anyela. Where I come from, this would be considered paradise at least, possibly even Heaven. I offer thanks to those of you responsible for my visit." She bowed slightly to the Guardian and looked for Hari and Sami in the crowd.

Dammit, they'd better be here for this, she thought, heart rate stepping up a couple of notches.

With a sigh of relief she glimpsed two tall heads making a ripple through the crowd and within seconds, Hari and Sami were at the front with, not surprisingly, Debalhi and Pemalina at their sides.

Alana drew in another breath.

"I have learned much from your genies, and also from you—kind people. You are possessed of a giving and loving nature, you welcome strangers and make them friends, and you sincerely care about each other. If I am to accept your graduation ceremony and all it entails, *I* can do no less."

Should she try President Kennedy's "I am an Anyelan" speech? Nah, they might not be Democrats.

"So, in the spirit of Anyela, I ask a boon of your Guardian."

A murmur rumbled through the crowd, and Hari and Sami remained motionless, gazes fixed on the figure in the vibrant yellow robe.

"I ask that, if I am successful in completing the graduation requirements and correcting my particular deviation in the time-line, that my tutors, Hari and Sami, be released from the genie program and allowed to become full citizens of Anyela."

Hari and Sami paled. Their women grasped the nearest hand and clung on for dear life. The rest of the crowd muttered and mumbled and discussed Alana's request, until the Guardian raised his hand again and silence fell.

"Alana West. You have shown the strength of commitment to your goals by your refusal to immediately accept our offering, and courage in enduring the punishment that you incurred. Your request is of a loving and unselfish nature. We are proud and happy to be able to grant it."

Cheers and clapping began somewhere in the crowd, and within moments everyone was jumping, yelling, cheering, waving and shouting their approval.

Pemalina and Debalhi stood with tears flowing down their faces, and Hari and Sami were speechless.

They moved as one to stand before Alana.

"You did this for us?" asked Hari roughly.

"This was your plan, to free us?" said Sami, choking back his emotions.

"How could I do less?" said Alana, holding her arms wide.

They folded her in a warm hug and held her tightly, neither man trusting his voice. She felt a sob run through somebody and a sniff from the other one.

"Hey guys, that's enough. You've got wonderful ladies waiting for you..." She eased back from their arms, uncaring that the tears were flowing down her cheeks.

"Go and be happy. Have kids, let *them* torture you. Have a life now, not a series of affairs. I have but one request..." she leaned toward them and whispered something. Then she kissed them both again and said "Just don't forget me..."

She deliberately turned away from them even though it was the hardest thing she'd ever done.

Alana gained strength from the gaze of the Guardian—he was approving her and encouraging her, and probably seducing her a bit too, because those black eyes of his were making her nipples get all uppity...

With a deep breath she stepped forward.

"I am ready for the Graduation Ceremony, Guardian," she announced.

A blast from some trumpets somewhere made her jump.

"Will the Qualifiers please step forward?"

As before, about fifteen or twenty delicious men moved into a line before Alana and dropped their silks.

Her mouth watered, her palms began to itch, and all over her body little hormones were standing up and fidgeting at this lovely presentation of some of the best dicks in the galaxy.

"Alana, any of these men would be deeply honored to share the Ecstasy Bed with you. As you know, your passions will make the flowers bud out on the tree—and this is considered an excellent demonstration of the continuation of our high standard of sexual skills, and also a general good-luck omen for Anyela as a whole."

Alana wandered up the line of hopeful cocks. Most impressive, she thought to herself, as they were obviously rising to the occasion.

"I may select any of these men?"

"Any of the men here before you are candidates, yes, Alana."

"Hmmm."

She walked down the line again, enjoying the sight of so many different men presented for her delight. She idly ran her palm from her shoulder down over her nipple to her waist, and silently chuckled as at least eighty percent of the cocks twitched and grew even more. This was the most fun she could remember having with clothes *on*.

"Hmmm."

The Guardian had no idea that when she made that sound, Alana was at her most dangerous, or thinking deeply, which often amounted to the same thing.

Stopping in front of a tall and bronzed man with a head of long red hair and a dick to match, she smiled, noting the answering grin in his deep green eyes. Oh my.

She turned and stepped up onto the dais next to the Guardian.

"I have made my selection," she announced and the crowd again fell quiet.

"You have indicated that I may select any candidate who stands before me today— and these are all exquisite men, any one of whom I would be glad to welcome to my bed."

She smiled politely at the assorted packages that were proudly displayed for her delectation. What a Kodak moment, she thought.

She turned and faced the Guardian, placing her hand on his hard chest.

"I choose you."

Chapter Twenty

Once again, Alana's words had brought an eerie silence to the town square. Then a chuckle started somewhere, and was followed by a guffaw from somewhere else. Within seconds the crowd was collectively clutching its stomach and rolling with laughter.

The Guardian was staring at Alana—she hoped that he might, in fact, be speechless. His expression was certainly indicating that he was in shock, if the dropped jaw and the round eyes were anything to go by.

"Me?" he squeaked, then coughed, clearing his throat.

"Yes, you. Is there a problem with that? Are you not able to—er—fuck?" Alana darted a teasing glance at his crotch. "If you aren't capable of helping me make the flowers bloom, then of course, I shall select another. I'm sure your people will understand and sympathize," she smiled wickedly.

Realizing that she was two seconds away from verbally emasculating him in front of a good portion of his people, the Guardian pulled himself together and raised his hand for silence.

Alana could have sworn she heard a familiar pair of snickers just as silence fell but didn't dare look over at Hari and Sami.

"Alana has made her selection. Although it is unique and has never been done before." He slanted a fiery gaze at her. *Oh boy,* she thought, *this is gonna be something else.*

"I, your Guardian, agree to lie with Alana West beneath the Ecstasy Tree. Then we shall see if the flowers will bloom and bring blessings to Anyela."

Cheers went up at this announcement, and the Guardian slid his arm around Alana's waist and pulled her to him — hard.

"And you'd better be ready for the ride of your life, woman," he hissed through a smile. "I'm going to fuck you until not only the Ecstasy Tree blooms but every other tree on Anyela does as well, along with a few forests on nearby planets."

"Bring it on, Guardian — I can't wait."

"We shall retire to the Ecstasy Tree," he said to the crowd. "Let all those who wish to, also retire — this day is henceforth decreed as a day of pleasure for all."

The crowd roared its approval, and the Guardian pulled Alana against his hard body. Bending her over his arm he kissed her, long, hard and with lots of tongue — romance novel cover artists would weep with envy, thought Alana, as she considered the picture they made — Mr. Tall-Dark-and-Droolworthy laying one enormously sexy smooch on Miss Sliding-Around-In-Silk.

His hand slipped inside her robe and caressed her breast — God, was he going to start here in front of gazillions of horny Anyelans? Her heart thumped — if he kept kissing her like this, he could start wherever and whenever he wanted, she thought, as she felt her brain closing down and diverting all incoming messages to her pussy.

"You asked for it, my delight," he said, sweeping her up into his arms.

"Oh yeah," she grinned.

* * * * *

The Ecstasy Tree sat at the edge of the lake, trailing mammoth roots out into and beneath the water. It was surprisingly ordinary, thought Alana, as the Guardian navigated the small path that led through an archway into a secluded garden. The array of branches that created the bed was a couple of feet off the ground, and had been covered for the occasion with silk quilts and pillows.

The Guardian dropped her on it.

"Ooof," she said, landing hard.

"You are very daring, Alana West," muttered the Guardian as he struggled to get his tunic off his shoulders. Suddenly he seemed all thumbs.

Alana giggled and came up on her knees, helping him slide the black silk off his wonderful shoulders and onto the cool grass that carpeted the bower.

He stilled as Alana's hands went to his trouser fastening and slid the cord free.

His pants joined his tunic on the grass, and Alana got her first good look at what had to be one of nature's masterpieces.

His cock was growing as she smoothed her hands around it, thick and well formed, it lay just perfectly across her palm.

The head was sculptured, flaring and elegant, with a finely carved ridge and an obviously sensitive spot underneath, which brought a hiss from the Guardian's lips as she ran a fingertip over it gently.

She lowered her head and flicked her tongue lightly across the tip, watching for his reaction.

A soft moan made her smile. Gotcha.

Hoping that Hari and Sami had done what she asked, Alana eased away from the Guardian's cock with a final stroke, which included his balls hanging comfortably between his beautifully muscular thighs.

He followed her down onto the bed.

"My turn," he muttered, pulling her belt open and stripping her robe away from her body in about two seconds flat.

He gazed at her for long moments.

"I begin to envy my genies, Alana," he smiled, running a fingertip around her navel and making her shiver.

"Your skin is so soft, and your body just made for fucking." He bent his head to her breast and she felt the light caress of his hair as it tumbled onto her skin like tiny fingers of sensation.

His tongue teased and tormented her nipple for what seemed like hours, until with a pop he released it and leaned over to repeat the process on the other breast. Her pussy was quivering and she could feel herself getting hot and wet.

Her hips moved automatically, encouraging him to get where he belonged.

A smile crossed his face.

"Not yet, anxious one. This is going to take some time…" He licked and suckled her strongly, rubbing his hands from her wrists up the sensitive skin underneath her arms and over her body.

Her nipples, aroused and darkened, were glistening from his mouth, eagerly demanding more attention.

Alana knew she had to get some control back, or she was going to succumb way too early to this marvelous lover and his amazing tongue. And she hadn't even gotten to the best part of him yet.

With surprising strength, she pushed his shoulder and rolled him onto his back, keeping her thighs tight around his hips as she did so.

Now she was on top, riding him, her moist clit poised between his legs, his cock resting against her belly. She smiled, and tried for the enigmatic Mona Lisa look. It might not have been tremendously successful seeing as her internal organs were simmering close to the boil, but she did her best.

"There is much time, as you said, Guardian." She glanced around and saw that her genies had come through for her — a little table was next to the bed and on it was a pot with a golden label.

"I would like to honor you with a treat from my world which is said to enhance lovemaking," she said formally, watching his eyes.

A brow raised high at her words, but he said nothing, just lay there gazing at her. She might have thought he was unaffected at her words, had not his cock twitched and given him away. Gotcha again.

She leaned over to the table, picked up the warm pot, and brought it over to sit carefully on his chest.

She dipped a finger in and brought it out dripping with melted chocolate. She gently smeared it over her nipple, taking her time to cover the areole, and then moving to the other side and doing that one as well.

There was considerable cock twitching as she tended to her nipples. *Oh boy, you are SO mine*, thought Alana with glee.

Moving the pot to the side, Alana leaned forward, dangling one chocolate-tipped breast near the Guardian's mouth.

"Taste me, Guardian," she breathed.

His cock did a genital version of the pole vault.

Hesitantly, he raised his head slightly and licked at her nipple. He paused, savored the taste and then came back for more. Considerably more. He cleaned both breasts in seconds flat.

"What is that?" he asked, licking his lips.

"We call it chocolate, which means 'food of the gods'," she ad-libbed. "Let's try this."

She dipped again and painted the Guardian's flat nipples with a healthy swipe of the sauce. Bending over, she gently and thoroughly cleaned them off with her tongue, swirling and nibbling as she went and bringing him to a quivering mass of sensation as she did so. She tried to remember every little flick that Sami had used to such good effect on her, and it seemed to be working.

The Guardian was breaking out into a sweat.

"Now of course, we could try this," she breathed, stroking her fingers in circles around his navel.

He groaned.

She lapped and licked.

He sighed.

"And for the *piece de resistance*..." she slid down and began painting his cock with long smooth strokes, balls to tip, until he looked like a pornographic Tootsie Roll. And oh, did he taste good. She lingered, licking the base thoroughly, nibbling at little bits of hardened chocolate that had dropped to his balls. A gentle swipe with her tongue cleaned them thoroughly and she continued to make her way upwards around this throbbing, chocolate-coated wonder. The sweet candy and the salty man mixed into a unique flavor in her mouth—she was practically drooling by the time she reached the head. A drop of moisture beaded at the tip and she relished it like the most delectable treat, massaging his balls gently as she flicked the last of the chocolate off the head.

He moaned, his veins standing out in an effort to control his orgasm, and he grabbed her head to pull her away.

"Not yet, Alana...We have to make the tree bloom. That means both of us, love, together."

He flipped her over, grabbed her hips and thrust deeply into her soaking cunt.

She moaned as his cock learned her innermost textures, and gasped as he slid out of her, only to return even deeper.

He was huge, filling her tightly and pressing somewhere in the vicinity of her tonsils.

He reached for the little pot of chocolate.

"Now let me see," he murmured.

She writhed, wanting that wonderful cock doing its job—soon, now, ten minutes ago.

"Oh no, no, greedy one. It's my turn to honor *you*," grinned the Guardian.

His powers of self-control must have been quite outstanding, thought the small clinical part of Alana's mind that was still vaguely functioning.

He spread the chocolate over her breasts, teasingly ignoring the nipples, then licked it off, each harsh swipe of his tongue traveling over the sensitive buds.

She keened, high in her throat.

He smeared her navel and razed the hardening crust off with his teeth, sending goosebumps all the way to her toes.

Then he eased himself out of her cunt and pushed her thighs wide.

"Time to add some special ingredients, I think," he muttered.

Easing away from her a little, he dipped his fingers once again in the melted chocolate, scraping the last of it from the pot.

Alana held her breath, knowing she'd have a hard time withstanding this dual assault, fingers and chocolate, which began to make its way to her pounding clit.

His fingers were sure and firm, the chocolate was warm, and Alana could feel an internal fuse getting shorter and shorter.

He paused for a moment, waiting for the chocolate to harden. Then, he bent his tongue to her.

Carefully, he nibbled away at her labia, cleaning, smoothing, lapping, always nearer and nearer to her clit, but never quite on it.

She grabbed her bottom lip between her teeth and held on, desperate to keep her orgasm at bay as long as she could.

Her clit was almost painfully aroused when his tongue finally arrived at its target. Two quick swirls and a swipe and Alana knew it was beyond her control.

She opened her mouth to draw breath into her starving lungs as the muscles in her legs and thighs began to tighten and the Guardian, sensing her condition, grabbed her buttocks with his hands and thrust his face into her pussy to make sure that she was right where he wanted her.

Oh, she was. The ripplings began, fierce, shattering, clenching, wiping Alana's mind free of all conscious thought.

Her body spiraled up, up toward a glittering target somewhere in an alternate universe, and as the mighty spasms began, the Guardian raised himself up along her body and thrust home.

Alana screamed out, lost in the bliss of his huge cock inside her as her cunt rhythmically squeezed him tight.

After several moments (or possibly eons), she realized that he'd begun to move, the shadows of her orgasm remained, and he was now urging her on.

Was there anyplace else to go? Shouldn't they both be little sodden and exhausted lumps of sticky flesh by now?

Apparently not. The Guardian was moving faster and faster, barely brushing her extraordinarily sensitive clit with his body, his balls slapping firmly against her buttocks.

He shifted his hips slightly, and she found that his cock was brushing something inside her—oh, God. Something so exquisitely sensitive that she was beginning to spasm all over again, but from inside this time.

Damn the man—all these years, and she'd believed the G-spot was a myth. Obviously, the G stood for Guardian.

His buttocks pistoned harder and faster and her breath came in fits and starts, her hands grasped the soft quilts as she writhed beneath him.

"Alana," he commanded, through clenched teeth. "Alana — it's time…"

Incapable of forming coherent words, Alana opened her eyes. She gazed into the Guardian's face above her, letting her expression do her talking.

His own eyes were black and blazing, his lips drawn taut, and sweat rolled down the side of his face to his shoulders. He was beautiful.

"Now, come NOW."

With a final ramming thrust that should have removed her wisdom teeth, the Guardian erupted, and the volcanic pulsations of his cock threw her over the edge and into another amazing orgasm.

She heard someone screaming and realized it was her.

She heard someone crying out, and realized it was him.

God, they were making a lot of noise.

She felt his warm cum spurting inside her endlessly, caressing her clenching muscles and bathing her womb. Her entire existence seemed focused on their joining, this one perfect moment in time when all life, as she knew it, had become centered on this incredible fuck.

With a last twitching shudder, the Guardian collapsed onto her damp body, and rolled to one side.

She looked at him, and wondered at the gentleness she saw on his relaxed face. He smiled.

She raised her eyes and gasped.

The entire tree above them was covered in enormous blue blossoms. The petals were trembling and a few were beginning to fall on the entwined lovers beneath.

"We did it," she breathed, surprised that words could actually come out of her mouth.

"You did it, Alana," whispered the Guardian, pulling her close into his body. "You did it."

Chapter Twenty One

Something long, smooth and hard was poking Alana.

"Hari, cut that out," she moaned, lifting her leg slightly so that he had better access.

A low chuckle greeted her words.

"Okay, Sami, you'd better make this good, I'm still half-asleep," she muttered.

"Try again, Alana-love," said the deep voice behind her.

Struggling to consciousness, Alana turned her head slightly and looked into a pair of black, glittering eyes, which were burning as he slid his cock home.

"Aahh…" he sighed. "That is good. You're so hot and tight and ready for me, aren't you, Alana?"

"G-G-Guardian?" she stuttered, fighting the onslaught of his fingers tickling her clit, his cock smoothly plunging into her and the warmth of his breath on her ear.

"I'm here," he said, as if there was any question in Alana's mind.

"You sure are," she sighed, relaxing into his talented body and allowing her pleasure to take over.

Within minutes he was fucking her into mindless bliss, cock deep within her, fingers strumming her swollen and tender clit.

This was no protracted lovemaking. This was a wonderful, get-the-systems-up-and-running, better-than-coffee, morning fuck.

Alana's cry of satisfaction as her orgasm hit her and rolled around her body was echoed by the Guardian's grunt as he pushed himself in deeper than ever and came.

Alana stayed right where she was, feeling the Guardian's cock relax in her cunt and loving his warmth down her spine.

She gave a little sigh of contentment and stroked his arm lazily.

Then, she realized something.

"I'm home," she said, looking around and seeing the familiar walls of her bedroom. "This is my room. We're not in Anyela any more."

She turned slightly as he slid wetly out of her body in a cloud of blue fog and sighed.

"Why are you here with me? What happened with the tree? Where's Hari and Sami? Oh lord, blue fog. You too?"

The Guardian pressed two fingers to her lips with a smile. She tasted herself on his hands—it was arousing as all heck, but she was teetering on the edge of hysteria—certainly not a good time to be thinking about a twofer.

"I brought you home, Alana. After the Ecstasy Tree bloomed—and I should tell you that no one can *ever* remember seeing it bloom like that—you had fulfilled all your graduation requirements—I think your term is 'in spades'?"

The Guardian grinned.

"I can assure you that my people will be talking of your powers and the good omens you created for many years to come. You may well become a legend on Anyela."

She reached out and tentatively touched his cheek.

"Hey, I couldn't have done it alone," she said.

Smiling widely, he leaned over and placed a smacking kiss on her lips.

"It's that sort of comment that makes you special, Alana-delight," he said. "Had we time, I'd show you just *how* special—" His knee slid between her thighs and opened them wide, allowing the cool air to brush against her hot cunt.

She sighed and squirmed a little.

"But I have things to tell you before we go any further. You asked about Hari and Sami." He eased them both up the bed until they were resting on the pillows, Alana's head tucked into his shoulder.

Waving his hand, a cloud of blue fog appeared at the bottom of the bed, rapidly solidifying into sort of a projection screen.

Images began to appear, cloudy at first, and then crystallizing into focused clarity.

Alana gasped as she recognized Hari, tumbled on a large blanket with Pemalina in his arms. They were enjoying one of those sensational Hari-kisses.

"Should we be watching this?" she asked the Guardian, feeling strangely bereft as she watched Hari's hand slip under Pemalina's robes.

"Sshh…" said the Guardian, hugging her close.

"Papa, Papa..." A child's voice broke the silence of the scene, and Hari rose up on one elbow to straighten Pemalina's skirts.

"Over here, scamp," he called.

Alana's jaw dropped as a miniature version of Hari dashed into the picture and threw himself onto his father.

"Where's your sister?"

"Wiv Unca Sami..." answered the tot, snuggling into his father's arms.

Sami appeared, holding a well-wrapped bundle in one arm and a very-pregnant Debalhi in the other.

"It is splendid practice for us, Hari—she's been as good as gold—let us change her, and everything," said a beaming Sami, as he gently lowered his burden into Pemalina's arms.

"Right, just double everything and you'll have it all down perfectly," said Hari teasingly.

"Well, we may have waited a while, but having two at once makes up for it, don't you think?" He lowered Debalhi carefully into a chaise and sat on the grass next to her feet, absently massaging her ankles and calves as he spoke.

Pemalina had extricated her little daughter from her blankets and was teasing smiles and gurgles from the baby.

Alana felt tears prickle her eyes as she watched, an unseen observer to this idyllic scene.

"Your wish was granted, Alana—Hari and Sami are free to be husbands, fathers— productive members of Anyelan society. In fact, Hari has bought his own vineyard-- already his wines are becoming much prized.

Sami has taken over his father-in-law's rug business and is also doing well. They will live long, happy lives surrounded by the ones they love, thanks to you."

Tears ran freely over Alana's cheeks as she watched the vision fade. She felt absolutely wonderful that she had accomplished so much, and completely shattered that it was over, and she was alone.

"Don't cry, love," soothed the Guardian.

"Do they — do they remember me?"

"Not as a person they taught, no. They honor you as the woman who came to Anyela and helped reorganize the genie program. They do not remember your time together. Although, interestingly enough, Hari's son is named Alan. I have often wondered…"

"How much time has passed, for heaven's sake? Have I been gone for years?"

The Guardian laughed.

"Time is only a concept, Alana," he said.

"Thank you, Stephen Hawking," she muttered, trying to cover her pain with sarcasm.

"You have just glimpsed a future timeline in Anyela — it has no reference to your time here in your world." He stroked a tangle of hair away from her face and tucked it behind her ear.

"That's how your genies were able to get that little pot of chocolate next to the Ecstasy Tree. A small time shuffle, and poof. Sex in a pot."

"They ratted me out, didn't they?" she grinned.

"On the contrary, they've done very nicely by setting up a little import business. Genie Candy is making a huge profit."

Alana laughed, feeling some of her pain lighten.

"And what about you, Guardian?" she asked, holding his hand tightly. "What happens to you?"

"We are not allowed to see our own future, Alana," he answered gravely. "That violates some of our most important principles. It is our sworn duty to guard the strands of time, not abuse the privilege."

"How long can you stay?" she asked, trying not to sound like a whining idiot.

"Not long," he answered. "There are many changes that must be dealt with in Anyela. Some are not happy with them — or me for allowing them."

"I'm sorry if I got you into trouble."

The Guardian's dark eyes met hers and fire burned in their depths. "I wish I had more time with you, Alana. If I could have anything I asked for, that would be my answer…"

She gently raised herself and kissed his lips.

"I shall miss you all — certainly Hari and Sami, but knowing they are happy makes the loss easier to bear. But you…that's another story." Her eyes filled with tears as she remembered his passion and his gentleness. "Will I remember anything?"

The Guardian ran his hands languorously up her thighs and cupped her mound. "Oh yes, Alana, there is much you will remember." His hand started a soft movement that had her sighing and opening her legs to him.

"You will remember that you are a deeply passionate woman with beautiful breasts…" His lips tugged on each nipple, making her moan.

"You will remember that loving yourself and who you are is very important, along with being proud of your strength and accomplishments…" His lips moved down to her navel.

"You will remember that fantastic sex needs an important ingredient—it needs your heart."

His head slid between her thighs and his tongue entered her.

She thrashed and groaned, held still by the firm grip of his fingers on her buttocks.

He kept his lips and tongue busy as one hand slipped from her buttock to her cleft and caressed her tightly puckered little anus.

She gasped with pleasure.

"You will also find gifts from us," he mumbled, raising his head and blowing on her hot and swollen clit.

She nearly shrieked with the pleasure of it.

"But most of all, you will find love, Alana, very soon…it is your destiny. You have changed more than you could possibly imagine…"

And with those words, he returned to her pussy and allowed his tongue to bring her to a shaking, trembling, ass-clenching orgasm.

She collapsed beneath him as he rose above her, smelling of Blue Lotus, sex and sweat. He dropped light kisses onto her eyelids and she slept.

Epilogue

The buzzing of an alarm clock woke Alana.

"Damn—it's Sunday, what's the matter with me?" she muttered, reaching for the offending appliance.

The buzzing continued.

"Aargh—the doorbell."

Staggering out of bed, she grabbed her black silk robe, trying fuzzily to knot the belt around her naked body. Her gold slave bell jingled and slapped her clit—as good a wake up call as any.

She shrugged and headed for her front door.

Her feet registered the incredible softness of the beautiful rug beneath her feet— maybe she could get another good deal from that guy who'd come by the store last year. This one was certainly a gem.

The morning sun sparkled on her favorite antique— her Murano glass Blue Lotus flower, which sat front and center in her display case.

The doorbell reclaimed her attention.

Looking through the peephole, she saw a nice chest. A very nice chest, definitely male, and covered in a pale green t-shirt. Hmmm.

She opened the door without releasing the chain.

"Hello?"

Her gaze traveled up to meet a twinkling set of the darkest eyes she'd ever seen. A mop of unruly midnight hair, streaked with silver over the ears, and a tidy moustache and goatee completed the handsome face. His grin was charming enough to melt butter.

"Hello. Are you Alana West?" His voice was husky with a slight touch of an accent. She couldn't quite place it.

"I'm Paul Guardino—I moved into George's apartment last night, only to find I have no electricity this morning and no number for the utility company. He left a note suggesting that you might be a good person to contact if I needed any help..."

Alana was staring at him, just enjoying the view.

Oh God, he'd stopped talking. She was supposed to reply—what the hell had he been saying?

"Um...sure, happy to help out, just a sec..." She pushed the door almost shut and removed the chain.

"Won't you come in?"

"That's very kind of you. Say..." A slight wrinkle pulled his dark brows together. "Have we ever met before? There's something awfully familiar about you." He laughed suddenly, a warm and happy sound. "God, that's such an awful line. I'm sorry I really did mean it..."

Alana grinned back. She couldn't help it—there *was* something familiar about this man, something that tickled her innards into doing a tango!

She closed her eyes for a second as his scent crossed the space between them. A wave of dizziness swept over her, and a flickering image of some kind of blue-flowered tree popped into her mind. Boy, she *really* had to stop eating cheese curls and cold pizza late at night!

"I'm about to make coffee, Mr. Guardino. Would you care for a cup?"

"Thanks, that would be lovely, but I don't want to disturb you..."

Too late, thought Alana, *waaaay too late*.

And she smiled.

Meanwhile, seven hundred and twenty-nine years into the future:

Major Boralle North is contemplating her next assignment — shore leave and participation in the sexuality games on Frallien IV. She's hesitant to register — the honor of her crew may well rest on her performance, and she doubts if it will be anything near their expectations. To put it bluntly, she is a sexual dud.

Her wanderings have brought her to a small marketplace, and she spies a little antique table — always fascinated by things from the past, she crosses the street and surveys the articles displayed for customers.

"I think I may have something you would find interesting, Major," says a smooth voice from behind her. Turning, she looks directly into a pair of vivid turquoise eyes. They belong to a tall, elegant human with long hair braided tightly at the back of his head, and who is holding out an unusual vessel for her attention — it has *one* very strangely shaped handle...

Enjoy this excerpt from
The Sun God's Woman
© Copyright Sahara Kelly 2002

Prologue

The lights in the conference room dimmed and the polite babble of conversation diminished to an expectant hush. The dulcet tones of the moderator swirled around the guests.

"Ladies and gentlemen, it is my pleasure to present our keynote speaker this evening. From Pendrake Industries, here to tell us about his exciting new discoveries, may I ask you to join me in welcoming Dr. Kyle Pendrake."

An enthusiastic round of applause greeted this comment, and in the back row of the room Annie Lynden caught her breath.

He was gorgeous.

He was one hot babe-magnet whose pictures hadn't done him justice.

And he was a dedicated scientist who had made magic. Literally.

There were some quiet moments while Dr. Pendrake's assistant carefully hooked up the small computer system next to the podium.

Annie's mouth watered as she used the time to study the notorious Dr. Pendrake.

Easily topping six feet, his hair was dark and longer than fashionable. Today he had tied it back neatly, but there were still fiery glints shining through when he bent to straighten a cable.

His clothes were neat and well tailored, and reeked of expensively casual chic. His round-necked shirt was definitely a silk knit, and was topped by a jacket that probably had been custom made for his broad shoulders.

Tasteful khakis fell in perfect creases to his gleaming loafers.

Not a pocket protector in sight.

He stood and glanced around the audience, and Annie caught a flash of light from incredible green eyes.

Sheesh, he was sex on a stick. She dropped immediately into a fantasy of licking her tongue up the sensitive flesh just inside his very naked hipbone. And back down. And over slightly.

A tap on the microphone brought her attention back to reality, although to judge by the parted lips and squirming bodies of the few other women present, she wasn't the only one picking up the major sex vibes from this luscious set of walking hormones.

"Good evening."

His voice was as appealing as the rest of him. He should probably have a government warning stamped on his butt. Just thinking about his butt distracted Annie and she wrenched herself back to business—to take notes on the lecture for her editor.

It was a coup for her to be here, because this was very much an 'invitation-only' affair. There were some pretty impressive looking suits in the front rows, and even a military uniform or two. Her editor had sworn that this project would probably end up classified within months, and would have come himself, but his wife was due to produce a little editor any second, and he hated science anyway.

So here she was, Miss Junior Reporter, still months away from graduating with a degree in journalism, covering what promised to be *the* hot technological topic of the year—Kyle Pendrake's "Magic".

Developing a severe case of lust for the noted scientist wasn't going to help her write the feature article she'd been promised, or the spot on the front page where her byline would appear. Her palms started to sweat as she worked the first sentences in her mind...

Dr. Kyle Pendrake may have discovered magic, but in the eyes of many of his audience, he managed to create a little of his own at last night's symposium... Yeah, that would make a nice intro...oops, he was beginning his lecture.

Annie leaned forward, unwilling to miss a second of what this guy was selling. Whatever it was, she'd take some.

"Merlin." The word floated through the now-silent room like a wisp of fog. "A name synonymous with the forces of magic, the forces of nature, a command of the most fundamental elements of our existence."

The audience was hushed, all attention focused on the man at the podium. The lights struck his head and upper body, leaving much of the rest of him in shadow. A nice dramatic touch, thought Annie, and one that worked well when you looked as yummy as the good professor.

"Magic," he continued, meeting as many eyes in the audience as he could. This guy knew how to work a crowd.

"The premise that magic exists is not new. Scientists have played around with the idea for many years. At Pendrake Labs, however, we don't 'play'...we get serious!"

A quick smile moistened the panties of at least three women in the second row, judging by their reactions.

"The result of our research is here with me tonight. Ladies and gentlemen, it is my pleasure to present to you...Merlin." A wave of his hand and a click of the remote control button produced a spotlight focused on the small unit at his side. He passed his hand over it and it began to glow.

Infrared sensors, thought Annie, busily jotting down her impressions, and refusing to be seduced by the show.

"Merlin is an acronym, standing for 'Magical Energies Resonator and Linear Integration Network" board. Actually," another smile crossed his handsome face, "...it's more correctly known as M.E.R.L.I.N. dash B."

The large screen behind Dr. Pendrake lit up with the Pendrake logo and a sleek graphic of the name Merlin.

"In our labs, it's the SR388 unit, and in our system here, it's...well, it's pretty special."

A shade of excitement had crept into his voice, and Annie paused in her note taking to watch him. She could just make out a pulse beating at the base of his neck as he turned to his unit, and a faint sheen of sweat was beginning to film his forehead.

A period of very technical information followed, which Annie wisely let slip by. Her readers wouldn't care about the operating system, whether it would work on the latest PC, or MAC, how many bazillion gigs of memory it needed, or whether Microsoft would be releasing a bug update within the promised time frame.

No, her readers wanted the whole picture...the images of what she was seeing, the end result of what this machine was rumored to do.

His scientific presentation winding down, Dr. Pendrake laid his notes back onto the podium.

"You are probably all a little bit curious about MERLIN." He smiled. "We were too, when we realized what we had developed. A plug-in board that can harness every bit of magic that is lurking near it. And there is magic everywhere, ladies and gentlemen, make no mistake."

He crossed to the front of the small dais and raised the lighting in the room with another click of his remote control. He could now see his audience more clearly, and the feeling of intimacy was heightened as he swept his gaze over the forty or fifty faces that intently watched him.

Annie felt his glance like a bolt through her body. His eyes hesitated a moment as they passed over her, and she felt the pull of his attraction right down to her thong! Sheesh, what she wouldn't give for a night with this guy. No holds barred.

"There is magic in the materials we use to create our buildings, and magic in the earth they stand upon. There is magic in the plants that grow, the wind that blows, and the air we need to sustain our very lives. "

I'll just bet there's some pure magic in your shorts, too, buddy, thought Annie.

His gaze flickered back to her, and for a second Annie was aghast at the idea he might have heard her. She blushed fiercely.

"This magical energy is collected by our friend MERLIN, and converted into digital impulses. The result?"

After a suitably dramatic pause, the monitor behind Dr. Pendrake lit up with some kind of movie. There were carriages moving up and down a busy street, and people bustling about their business. But unlike old films, this one was in glowing color and the movements of the crowds were natural.

"A viewer, if you will. A glimpse through the veils of time. An opportunity to *see* the past!"

There was complete and utter silence as mouths fell open and eyes widened. Unable to believe what she was seeing, Annie was as startled as everyone else.

"Yes, you are really looking at the past. We estimate this to be New York in about 1890 or so, judging from the clothing styles. I'll leave those details to the historians amongst you—our goal is to continue to provide opportunities to peek at our past, and to learn its secrets. MERLIN is truly a magician in that respect."

A murmur rose in the room as people started to question, wonder, puzzle, and in general react in a variety of ways to the outrageous claims made by Dr. Kyle Pendrake.

"I understand your shock. Believe me, the day we first discovered these amazing results, we were pretty much in shock too. But let me assure you that this is quite genuine. These images are being generated now, here, in this room, by the Merlin system. They are not recorded, digitized, enhanced or in any other way altered. You are seeing a moment in our history—as it happened."

The murmur rose to a hubbub as the scientists in the audience started firing questions at Pendrake, the historians struggled to get their hands on pencil and paper to note what they were seeing, the military whispered to each other, and a couple of women tried to get closer to the Professor.

Annie watched it all with skeptical eyes. Could it be possible? There had been a lot of ongoing research into the nature of magic and its presence, so that had a ring of truth to it. But capturing it? Turning a computer system into a wizard? And then casting a spell to create a window on the past?

This was all sounding way too much like a bad science fiction novel. If it hadn't been for the man on the dais who was expertly fielding questions, and the images playing on the huge monitor behind him, she might well have dismissed his claims as just another hokey experiment that was designed to rip people off.

But she could see the carriages rolling along the broad street, kicking up dust from the horses' hooves. As she watched, one horse deposited a large pile of steaming droppings and a woman crossing the street behind the carriage had to do some very fancy footwork to avoid it. Now *that* was realism.

The conversations around her continued, and many people had now moved closer to the unit and the dais.

Dr. Pendrake stepped back to allow them a chance to get a good look at his system. He moved away from the crowd and stood alone for a few moments. His eyes scanned the room and found Annie.

Once again, she felt something startling in his gaze. She knew he'd looked for her this time, and was not fooled into thinking it was because he'd developed a sudden case of lust for her body.

She was pretty much used to this reaction.

Her white-blonde hair separated her from her peers on a regular basis, and her unusual violet eyes finished the job. Why *she* had been born with the genetic flaw that resulted in albinism, she had no idea, and neither had her parents. In fact, it had been several years after her birth that her pediatrician had actually realized that Annie was an albino. She had the less severe form, and her eye color was proof of that. But her hair remained obstinately platinum, her eyebrows were practically non-existent unless she used her makeup properly, and she burned to a crisp at the beach.

Her glasses took care of her minor vision problems, and it really had been no hardship after she'd learned how to deal with it.

But it still attracted attention.

Just like the attention she was now getting from Dr. Hotbody.

She raised her chin slightly and held his gaze, refusing to look embarrassed that she hadn't joined the gushing throng of salivating techno-groupies. If he wanted her attention, he was going to have to come and get it.

Always assuming that she didn't drop to her knees and offer him whatever sexual favor he wanted. It would not further her image as a cool, calm, representative of the Fourth Estate. Drooling and humping his leg was probably out, too. She sighed as he turned away, summoned by a two-star general.

It had been a nice fantasy.

Returning to their seats, the crowd settled and waited for Dr. Pendrake to conclude his presentation.

"Well, you've had a chance to take a look at Merlin and what he can do. As I mentioned to some of you, we have only looked to the nineteenth century thus far, but tonight, in honor of your presence..." he bowed politely to his audience, "...we are going to set our parameters a bit farther back. Tonight we will attempt to sneak a glimpse into the age of Shakespeare, Sir Francis Drake, and the magnificent Virgin Queen herself, Elizabeth the First."

Incredulous gasps met this announcement, and an excited buzz of conversation covered Dr. Pendrake as he adjusted settings, typed in commands, and tapped nervous fingers on the data-crystal case in front of him.

He stood, and another tense silence fell.

The monitor grew blurry and the images of Victorian New York pixilated into darkness. The room lights dipped, and for a moment nothing but the glow of the LCD screen illuminated the faces staring at it.

Then all hell broke loose. A picture appeared. It was of the ocean, and sailing upon that ocean, two enormous galleons. The picture panned around to the wharves along the oceanfront. There were sailors meandering to and fro, barrels, crates, casks and ropes piled everywhere, and women walking — in enormous gowns.

Cheers and applause and cries of surprise and wonder erupted through the conference room.

 He'd done it.

Grinning from ear to ear, Kyle Pendrake also stared at the screen.

The crowd stood in unison, and Annie joined them. She was applauding as loudly as anyone and adding a couple of whistles to the cacophony. The excitement was infectious and the enthusiasm enormous.

Annie stood on a chair to watch Pendrake's reaction, and as she did, she noticed the Merlin unit next to him. It was vibrating slightly, its glow changing from a soft blue to more of an electric green. The greater the applause, the greater the change.

The size of its aura was getting larger too. Annie frowned and stopped clapping as she wondered if she should bring it to anyone's attention.

But the crowd, as the saying goes, went wild. Cheers brought out more cheers, and shouts of "Bravo" and "Magnificent" were tossed around with the applause.

The green glow was intensifying, now shining onto Pendrake's expensive khakis. There was a golden center to it, surrounding the unit, and it was pulsating. Annie realized that it was pulsating in time with the roar of the crowd.

They were the ones producing the energies that were feeding Merlin. It was eating their emotions, and liking them from the looks of it.

Little sparkles started flashing through the glow and suddenly Kyle Pendrake looked over at his creation. He froze for a second, then moved casually toward it.

God, was it going to explode?

Annie held her breath as the others continued their approbation, probably not realizing that this wasn't part of the show. The images had faded on the monitor, and the biggest source of light was now Merlin itself.

A woman, who hadn't taken her eyes off Pendrake all night, let out a loud yipping cheer, and Merlin lapped it up.

A giant fireball of light swelled around the unit, enveloping Kyle as he reached to disconnect the power.

There was a sudden hiss, followed by a screech of deafening proportions.

And Kyle Pendrake was gone...

About the author:

Born and raised in England not far from Jane Austen's home, reading historical romances came naturally to Ms. Kelly, followed by writing them under the name of Sarah Fairchilde. Previously published by Zebra/Kensington, Ms. Kelly found a new love - romanticas! Happily married for almost twenty years, Sahara is thrilled to be part of the Ellora's Cave family of talented writers. She notes that her husband and teenage son are a bit stunned at her latest endeavor, but are learning to co-exist with the rather unusual assortment of reference books and sites!

Sahara welcomes mail from readers. You can write to her c/o Ellora's Cave Publishing at 1056 Home Avenue, Akron OH 44310-3502.

Why an electronic book?

We live in the Information Age—an exciting time in the history of human civilization in which technology rules supreme and continues to progress in leaps and bounds every minute of every hour of every day. For a multitude of reasons, more and more avid literary fans are opting to purchase e-books instead of paperbacks. The question to those not yet initiated to the world of electronic reading is simply: *why?*

1. *Price.* An electronic title at Ellora's Cave Publishing and Cerridwen Press runs anywhere from 40-75% less than the cover price of the <u>exact same title</u> in paperback format. Why? Cold mathematics. It is less expensive to publish an e-book than it is to publish a paperback, so the savings are passed along to the consumer.

2. *Space.* Running out of room to house your paperback books? That is one worry you will never have with electronic novels. For a low one-time cost, you can purchase a handheld computer designed specifically for e-reading purposes. Many e-readers are larger than the average handheld, giving you plenty of screen room. Better yet, hundreds of titles can be stored within your new library—a single microchip. (Please note that Ellora's Cave and Cerridwen Press does not endorse any specific brands. You can check our website at www.ellorascave.com or

www.cerridwenpress.com for customer recommendations we make available to new consumers.)

3. *Mobility.* Because your new library now consists of only a microchip, your entire cache of books can be taken with you wherever you go.

4. *Personal preferences are accounted for.* Are the words you are currently reading too small? Too large? Too...**ANNOYING**? Paperback books cannot be modified according to personal preferences, but e-books can.

5. *Instant gratification.* Is it the middle of the night and all the bookstores are closed? Are you tired of waiting days—sometimes weeks—for online and offline bookstores to ship the novels you bought? Ellora's Cave Publishing sells instantaneous downloads 24 hours a day, 7 days a week, 365 days a year. Our e-book delivery system is 100% automated, meaning your order is filled as soon as you pay for it.

Those are a few of the top reasons why electronic novels are displacing paperbacks for many an avid reader. As always, Ellora's Cave and Cerridwen Press welcomes your questions and comments. We invite you to email us at service@ellorascave.com, service@cerridwenpress.com or write to us directly at: 1056 Home Ave. Akron OH 44310-3502.

NEED A MORE EXCITING
WAY TO PLAN YOUR DAY?

ELLORA'S
CAVEMEN

2006 CALENDAR

COMING THIS FALL

Discover for yourself why readers can't get enough of the multiple award-winning publisher Ellora's Cave. Whether you prefer e-books or paperbacks, be sure to visit EC on the web at www.ellorascave.com for an erotic reading experience that will leave you breathless.

www.ellorascave.com

Printed in the United Kingdom
by Lightning Source UK Ltd.
123113UK00001B/30/A